THE cupcake dilemma

by

JENNIFER RODEWALD

WORDS THAT EDIFY

Rooted Publishing

The Cupcake Dilemma

Printed in the United States of America
First Printing, 2018
Edited by Dori Harrell of Breakout Editing

Cover Design by Jennifer Rodewald and
Roseanna White of www.RoseannaWhiteDesigns.com
Images from www.Pixabay.com

Published by Rooted Publishing
McCook, NE 69001

Chapter 1

Let me begin by stating this clearly. I was *voluntold*.

This is a very important point. I didn't go hunting for the baker's attention, even if his dark hair and eyes had beckoned me for a second look the first time I'd ever gone into the Sweet Tooth.

Okay, I looked more than twice.

That was only because I was taken off guard. You go into a cutsie boutiquish bakery and you expect a perky woman with a big white apron behind the counter, right? Well, that's what I expected. Instead, a man with almost black hair, and eyes nearly as dark, greeted me from behind the gleaming pastry case. With that big white apron.

"Hey there, what can I get you?" he'd asked that first day back in September.

A bib.

Yeah. I thought that because I was pretty sure drool was gathering at the corner of my mouth. Because of the cupcakes. I think. Or not.

Fine. It was because of Ian Connealy. But I'm absolutely certain I'm not the only woman in Rock Creek to have a saliva issue on account of the owner of the Sweet Tooth Bakery. I'm equally sure that the fact he was his own baker was the reason his business was doing so well.

I mean, yum.

The cupcakes are pretty spectacular too. In case you were wondering. But we're getting way ahead of ourselves. Or, rather, catching up on backstory that doesn't really matter at the moment. Yet. But just know, Ian Connealy is pretty easy on the eyes.

And also, just so you know, I didn't set up this little arrangement. Like I said, I was *voluntold*.

Chapter 2

I work at Rock Creek Elementary as a second-grade teacher. A first-year second-grade teacher in a community that was not my home until early August the previous calendar year. So there's some information you might need to backpocket, because here's the thing: I wasn't a small-town girl to begin with, and moving into a small-town world when you didn't come from that kind of context is intimidating.

In a city, you can blend. You become like the background colors on a Monet, and you just sort of…yeah. Blend. And it works for a fairly introverted girl like me—except, if I'm honest, there's a real downside to blending. It's not the same thing as fitting, and it can be lonely. There were other things about the city life that didn't work for me, so when my college advisor showed me the list of positions available in a more rural setting, I was interested. After all, what could be so scary about moving to a little town nowhere near any other little towns? It'd be cozy, right? No light pollution, no screaming sirens every single night, and hey! I wouldn't need to worry about carrying around that pepper spray my dad gave me on my sixteenth birthday.

Totally dreamy.

Yeah, so that cozy thing…it's a complete rumor. Straight-up misconception. And in other words, not true. Moving as the outsider into a small town full of insiders is massively conspicuous. I could have had a cone hat on my head labeled NEW IN TOWN and probably garnered the same amount of questioning looks. Mind you, they weren't mean looks, but looks nonetheless. See, while most people in Rock Creek are friendly, there is this invisible thing that binds them together in a way that makes a new girl feel…well, like an outsider. I doubt it's intentional, but it's hard to step over the unseen cord of *they've known each other since diapers and all graduated high school together*, especially when you've never had that kind of lasting connection with anyone in your life.

It's intimidating.

But I'd signed a contract, and truly, I liked this sweet little town. The main street is still paved with bricks, for goodness' sake. And they have a barn party in the middle of town for every major holiday, and a few minor ones as well. Not to mention the piñata at Christmas. That's the clincher, right there. *Everyone* should have a barn-party, piñata-breaking Christmas celebration. It should just be in the holiday rules.

So there I was, in love with a small town that I hadn't quite fit into yet, wrestling through my first year of teaching, which is *not* an eight-to-three job no matter what you see on the dumb television, and…

Single.

That last part gets noticed in a small town. The charming, double-edged sword of small-town thinking is that no one over the age of sixteen should be single. Ever. Homecoming dates are very, very, very important. And prom. And Valentine's. And…well, if you're out of school, um…

So…you're still single?

It's well meaning, I promise. And it's pretty understandable. In this little community, most people over the age of twenty are married, so naturally, the singleness is an anomaly. And naturally the sweet old ladies at church want to help with that anomaly. It's just expected.

What I didn't expect was for my principal, a married man in his early thirties with three kids of his own, to be worried about it.

Apparently, he was.

It went down something like this: Thursday mornings we have an all-school staff meeting. It's early—we're supposed to be in the cafetorium by 7:00 a.m., seated, with our coffee and bagels in hand (Mr. Hanson, the principal, supplies those), and ready to go through that week's agenda.

That week happened to be the first full week back to school after winter (insert *Christmas* here, if you're old school) break. We were pretty much exhausted, because kids coming back to school after a two-week break is a little bit like caging the monkeys after you've let them rule the zoo for a few days. They're not really in favor of that, and we were not exactly loving it either. Add to the madness, snow. Did you know that snow makes seven- and eight-year-olds nuts? I can't really explain it, but there's something in the chemistry of tiny frozen water droplets falling from the sky that seriously messes with their sweet little selves. They go crazy, and a room full of crazy second graders *might* have the propensity to make their first-year teacher crazy. Or just tired. Perhaps both.

Don't ask me how I know.

Apparently this crazy monkey-caging situation had worn on my colleagues as well. The pre-meeting murmurs had been littered with comments about needing double the coffee, and every adult in the room wore the *is it Friday afternoon yet?* expression. So when Mr. Hanson started the morning staff meeting with his normal *Good morning, Rock Creek Elementary superheroes!* we all kind of groaned our response.

"Ah, come on now. I've got the best staff in the state. Don't you think we've got the best staff in the state, Mrs. Anderson?"

Mrs. Anderson, our office secretary, painted up an enthusiastic grin that looked about as real as Dolly Parton's hair. "Absolutely. The best."

Mr. Hanson nodded, grinned wider, and faced us again. "I know. It's been a week. We've got Christmas-hung-over kids, snow brains, and it's not quite Friday, but we're in this together."

Pause here, because you should know, I really like our principal. He's here because he wants to be here. He's always interacting with the kids, and they adore him. Even if he has some unrealistic expectations about what his "superhero" staff can do, he really does believe in us—and what we're all here to do. So if this is coming off as sour, know that it's not. It's just the whole first-full-week-back-at-school thing, and also it's the *this guy totally set me up* thing. Even if it wasn't intentional. I haven't decided that part yet.

"I think we need to look forward to the upcoming excitement we have planned here in Rock Creek. That'll help us get over these first-week-back blues. So today, let's start by discussing our Valentine's Day plans. Huddle leaders, would you mind reporting what you've got planned, both for your classrooms and for our community?"

Huddles are simply grade-level teachers grouped together. Each grade has three, except the second grade. We have four, because apparently the year these kids were conceived, there had been a string of snowstorms in Rock Creek, resulting in a baby boom that fall. You would not believe how many kids have birthdays in September and October in my classroom.

Grade by grade, huddle leaders stood and reported.

Kindergarten planned to celebrate the holiday as one large group. They would use their kindergarten commons, where they would play hearts-and-arrows tic-tac-toe on the giant floor board, eat heart-healthy valentine-themed snacks, and make cards for the students' special people at home. For their community contribution, they were in charge of decorating the barn for this year's Valentine's Day barn dance.

Mr. Hanson nodded approvingly. "Well done, gang. First grade, you're up."

Anastacia Campbell stood to deliver her report. She's a beautiful woman—just a couple years older than me, and was also new to Rock Creek Elementary. The large diamond on her left hand and the sweet little baby bump poking from under her bohemian-styled tunic helped her to slide into Rock Creek life pretty easily. I think. It seemed so, anyway.

"We're so excited for this." She beamed, clearly over the whole *this first week back is rough* fog. "We've decided to take Valentine's Day on the road. We'll be going to the Care Center, bringing approved baked goods with us. We've also arranged for each student to interview a Care resident, and we'll prepare questions with them the week before so that they'll be able to get to know some of the residents. When we get back from the Care Center, we'll celebrate with some cookies and exchange our own valentines."

She clapped her hands and tucked them under her chin. I could almost hear Julie Andrews squealing *wheeee!* from the original *Sound of Music*. It was a great idea, so she had every right to beam.

"Excellent!" Drawing out each syllable of that word, Mr. Hanson was clearly impressed. "Classroom and community rolled into one. I love it."

Mrs. Campbell was totally getting educator of the year.

"Second grade, you're next."

Thankfully, I was not the huddle leader for second grade. Nolan Meyers, one of two men who taught at Rock Creek Elementary, stood to deliver our report. I kind of held my breath, because how were we supposed to follow the first-grade act?

Nolan cleared his throat and rubbed the back of his neck. "We've decided to go standard protocol. Room moms will be helping out, bringing snacks and games. The kids will spend the morning making their valentine boxes, and we'll exchange cards before breaking out the food."

"Ah." Mr. Hanson maintained a grin, but clearly we were a letdown.

Who knew first grade was going to go for gold on this? I didn't even know it was a contest, and here they were in it to win it.

"And community involvement?"

"Yeah. We're doing the food for the Valentine's Day dance. We'll hammer out the details as we get closer to the date, but right now I've got the lowdown on shredded beef sandwiches, brought to us by our ever-generous Kent family. We'll also be supplying drinks and desserts."

"Excellent." Mr. Hanson seemed to recover from the disappointment fall. "How about we just hammer out those details now? Nolan's got main dish covered. Martia, would you think about sides—and remember it's not all on you. Use your resources. And, Amy, can you manage drinks?"

Both nodded, because what else were we going to do? It worked.

"And Kirstin, desserts?"

Wait, what?

"Cupcakes are always a favorite," he continued, though I had sat there staring at him, surely with a deer-in-the-headlights kind of look on my face.

Was the man talking to me?

"Great, so that's settled. Third grade…"

Cupcakes? I'd just been assigned cupcakes? For a dance? A dance the *whole town* was going to attend? What was the man thinking? He'd been a part of our staff potlucks. Knew my standard fare. *Never once* had I brought baked goods, and there was a reason.

But he'd moved on. It was done. Which meant I couldn't get out of it. No matter how much of a failure I was in the baking world, I was bringing cupcakes to the Valentine's Day dance. And those sugary little devils would be representing Rock Creek Elementary's second-grade class.

No pressure.

Chapter 3

I have a kitchen because it came with the house. It's pretty hard to rent a little place without a kitchen, so I didn't even include *no kitchen necessary* on the wish list I'd given to Alice May, my real estate agent and town liaison, and also my first friend in Rock Creek.

In truth, a microwave and a sink would have been just fine. The rest of the kitchen amenities supplied in my adorable little bungalow are pretty much decorative features that make me look normal.

After a full day of stressing about the cupcake mandate, and some teaching mixed in with the part of my brain that I could force to focus like a mature adult, I headed home to my not-very-well-used kitchen and stared ruefully at the oven I'd never once turned on. I think I heard it laugh at me. The *mwhahahaha!* kind of laugh. Evil. Sinister. As if it was a dare. *Try it, kitchen-fail girl. Just try it…mwhahahaha!*

I glared at it. "You'll never take me alive!" (You get to talk to inanimate objects in your home when you live alone. I claim it as a perk.)

The oven's mockery intimidated me. I liked my cute little house. I didn't want to burn it to the ground taking on some dumb dare from a kitchen appliance. So naturally, I checked out *microwave cupcake recipes* on Google. There were a surprising number of options, and I embraced a moment of near-champion giddiness. Stepping off a little sassy sashay, I tossed a gleeful glance at my oven. "Not taking me down, baby. Not today."

I could totally pull this off—without the dumb oven—and my level of awesomeness with my second-grade class would climb a few more ticks north.

This is super important to a new teacher, and I think for the non-teachers out there I should just say it straight: we want our kids to think we're awesome. Our ability to dump information and life lessons into their spongy little short-attention-span brains rides significantly on whether or not they actually think we're pretty fantastic and know what we're doing in life. And our self-image also has a few hooks sunk into that opinion.

So I pulled down my single mixing bowl—which also doubles as a serving bowl when we have staff lunches. My standby is pasta salad—you know, the kind that you mix up from a box? There are microwave directions on that stuff, and as long as you remember to drain the excess water from the pasta before adding the mix-it-up-in-a-cereal-bowl dressing, it turns out pretty well. And as a bonus, if you throw in some cherub tomatoes and a cup of frozen peas, the obvious this-is-out-of-a-box presentation fades and you can claim that you "made" it.

After washing the mixing bowl, because it'd been a while since our last staff potluck lunch, I rubbed my hands together. There might have been a giddy little hop from my socked feet as I read through the set of directions on my iPad, because *woohoo! Cupcakes from the microwave!* Who knew?

I didn't have the baking powder the screen was telling me I needed. Baking soda, yes, because I keep it in my refrigerator—my mom says to do that because it absorbs odors—but powder, no. They're the same though, right? Both white powdery stuff used for baking. Right there in the name. *Baking.* So, same.

I measured the flour and sugar and other stuff and mixed, my teeth taking hold of the corner of my bottom lip in sweet anticipation. This was going to open up a whole new world for me. Baked goods. I could bring *baked goods* to the next staff lunch, and my gradual acceptance into the small-town culture would maybe take a shortcut. I didn't know why, but I was pretty sure it would.

When the batter looked…wet and batterish, I wiped my flour-dusted hands on my jeans and marched back to the iPad.

Muffin tin. I was supposed to spoon the batter into the muffin tin. What muffin tin? I didn't own a muffin tin. What was more, could a muffin tin go into the microwave? I was a microwave aficionado, and the word *tin* set off images of flying sparks, loud, scary popping sounds, and the acrid Kirstin-burned-something-again smell.

Muffin tin was a no-go. What else could I use? My coffee mug—but that thing was too big. However, my mom gave me a set of delicate-looking teacups that she'd inherited from her grandmother. They had about the right circumference. I could just run a knife around the edges of my finished cupcakes and pop those fluffy little bites of yumminess right out. In my mind, I pictured the whole thing—sliding the little cups out of my handy-dandy microwave, the delicious smell of creative success tickling through my nostrils, and then with a quick swipe and dump, my perfect little culinary creations would be ready to impress.

It'd work.

Then I'd call my mother. She might fall into delirious shock that her kitchen-fail daughter had stumbled onto such a genius solution. We would laugh, and she'd say "high five in the air, Kirstin," and I would smack the empty air with my palm, returning the gesture.

This was going to be fantastic.

That line kept repeating itself inside my brain while I spooned the batter into my great-grandmother's teacups, humming "We Are the Champions" with an obnoxiously loud voice. Another benefit of living alone.

The batter filled the four cups exactly. My instructions said to bake at 50 percent power for seven minutes. Just enough time for me to go fold the load of laundry that waited for me in the dryer, an amenity that I actually used and had also come with the house.

Somewhere between five and seven minutes, as I finished matching the final few pairs of socks, a loud *boom* reported from the direction of my kitchen. It sounded like a gunshot, and being the city girl that I was, I frantically searched my mind as to whether or not I'd kept that pepper spray my dad had given me all those years ago.

Boom! Another report. Followed by the sound of shattering glass and the telltale smell of smoke.

Forgetting about the pepper spray, I reached for the fire extinguisher—a housewarming gift from my mom, which I didn't think was nearly as funny as my sister did—and launched toward the kitchen. By the time I made the trip down the hall from the back of the house to the front, the smoke alarms were screaming at full blare. Smoke belched out of my microwave, whose door had burst open due to the explosion, and shattered pieces of heirloom teacups had scattered across the hardwood floor, mingling with black blotches of burned cupcake batter.

Mark it down, I thought. *Kitchen-fail number 362. Thousand.*

Note to grandmothers everywhere: do not give kitchen-fail granddaughters your heirloom teacups. It will not end well.

Thankfully, I didn't need the extinguisher. However, I was going to need a new microwave. And a different plan entirely.

Chapter 4

"Friday afternoon!" A week later, Anastacia Campbell floated into the copy room behind the front office of the school, a dramatic sigh contradicted by the unmistakable smile in her voice. "Wow, it's been a week. Anyone else?"

I was pretty sure she was talking to me, because I was the only one standing at the copy machine, waiting for Monday's spelling worksheet to finish replicating. It *had* been another challenging week. More snow and bitter cold had made the last full week of January long. The start of the new year was promising a noteworthy winter, and I wasn't sure the kids and I were going to survive. They were stir crazy, which had the potential to drive me plain crazy.

"Yeah." I smiled as I turned to her. She was stunning. Did I mention that before? If she could somehow manage to rein in her Princess Petunia Positivity neurosis enough to perfect a pouty slouch, Mrs. Campbell could model. Currently, for a maternity line. With her sweetly rounded baby bump and warm expectant-motherly glow, every pregnant woman in America would daydream about being as adorably sexy (is that possible?) as Mrs. Anastacia Campbell was.

"It's been a doozy," I added.

"Straight-up insanity." She chuckled. Like it was funny.

I wondered about the woman's insatiable perkiness. Did it only ooze out at school, or was her husband exposed to it on a regular basis as well? Not that that was a bad thing, just…unusual. And frankly, made me a little bit jealous. Maybe it was her brand of coffee?

"So…" I glanced at the copier, as if it needed me to check its progress, and then looked back at Anastacia Perky-Bell. "That was a pretty awesome idea your huddle came up with—taking Valentine's Day on the road."

"I know, right!" She sounded like Rapunzel on *Tangled*.

I may have pulled back just a tad, because, *whoa with the enthusiasm! There are no children around here to impress.* "Are you always this…"

"Happy?" She grinned. "Yes. Except not after ten. Mitch, my husband, says my perk-a-lator shuts down at ten."

I laughed. That was actually funny. "So it's not just a school face, huh?"

"Nope. I just have a lot of energy. It all comes out in smiles and squeals. Sometimes it's a little much, isn't it?"

The woman *did not stop* smiling through the whole exchange. I had to giggle again. "No, just not normal, is all. But it's a good oddity. I'm a little green about it."

She waved a hand at me. "Don't be. Mitch tells me I need a dial-down-the-positivity knob. I'm really bad in stressful situations. Hyper-positivity on belladonna. I'm all like, 'It's fine. It's all good. No worries, hon. It's gonna work out.' And he's like, 'Babe. The car is on fire. It's not all right. Stop being delusional.'"

I think I snotted a little as I burst out laughing. "For real? The car was on fire?"

Her perfectly white, straight teeth gleamed as her grin spread fuller. Not sure how that was possible, but anyway…

"It's a long story." Her eyes widened, as if she'd just had an epiphany. "Hey! Mitch is out of town this weekend. Want to hang out? I hate being home alone." She grabbed my arm and shook it a little. "Oh! Please say yes! I haven't had a girls' weekend in forever. Mitch and chick flicks aren't super-good friends, and he isn't a fan of chocolate. Isn't that so weird? Who doesn't like chocolate, right? But he's a good guy, so I overlook his strange quirks. We could watch a movie and eat junk—*chocolate*—and then tomorrow maybe we could meet at the Sweet Tooth. Want to?"

Pretty sure amusement wrote letter-by-letter over my expression. Didn't think she took a breath through any of that. Holy happiness, this woman was hilariously nuts.

She beamed, pretty sure she was using *the happy force* on me. "Say yes."

"Okay, yes."

A squeal filled the room—Rapunzel-style again. "Yay!"

The copier beeped, letting me know that it had finished the task without my oversight. How responsible of it. Grinning, I turned back to the machine, snatched my stack of Monday's educational plans, and turned back to Anastacia.

"Your place or mine?"

"Oh, I invited you over, so of course mine!" She hugged me.

I stood there stiff—mostly because I didn't see that coming and was too shocked to know what to do with it.

"We're going to have so much fun." One more squeeze and she stepped away. "510 West Third. We still have Christmas lights up—because I love them. Mitch says they have to come down by Valentine's Day. What a party pooper right? Anyway…seven?"

I nodded, shaking with silent laughter. "Seven."

"Eeee!"

I laughed again.

This woman…

I liked her. A lot. Especially because during that whole conversation, I didn't once think about the Cupcake Dilemma, which was a huge bonus. I'd been having nightmares about showing up at the dance with burned balls of batter slathered in runny, toothpaste-ish frosting that was more bitter than sweet. To make it worse, I would be standing in the middle of the barn wearing my wool socks and long underwear and the Christmas moose antlers my sister had given me. Everyone laughed, and Mr. Hanson fired me on the spot—right after he told me that I would never find a place in Rock Creek. The dream would go from ridiculously embarrassing to heartbreaking, and every time I'd tried to wake up before the horrible moment of his frowning dismissal, I would be trapped and forced to watch the scene play out. (Maybe that's too much information?)

Anyway. I didn't think of any of that while Anastacia and I talked. Not once.

I think I just scored a new friend.

I wondered how the car fire had worked out and hoped she'd remember to tell me that story. Or, I'd just ask because I felt like I needed to know. After all, if their car fire worked out, like she'd declared to her more feet-planted-in-reality husband, then my cupcake problems surely would be okay too.

Right?

***

Anastacia looked model worthy in yoga pants too. But I wasn't going to let that deter me from exploring this budding friendship, especially since she seemed almost as eager as I was to sift it out.

Okay, she was more. But chalk that up to personality. Eager came with the perkiness, so I had to take that into consideration. Even so, as we lounged on her couch, devouring fudge cheesecake with a Hallmark movie playing in the background, I sank into the sensation of blooming friendship. It was like the color pink. Happy and pretty and irresistible.

"So I was struggling in my second-year biology class, and I searched the campus listings for a tutor." Anastacia licked the remaining fudge off her fork and then continued. "Mitch's name came up, and I called him. He sounded so stern and nerdy over the phone, all 'Tell me where you're struggling most,' and 'Are you going to be serious about this, because I'm in premed and can't waste my time with some underclassman flirt.'"

I leaned forward from my corner of the couch Anastacia and I shared. "Na-huh, he said that?"

She tried—she really made a go-for-the-scowl effort—at frowning. "He. Did. The punk. I was so offended."

Yeah, she looked all offended with that permanent grin pushing up the corners of her mouth and the gooey girl-in-love gleam in her eyes.

"I told him," she continued, about three blocks away from pulling off serious, "'*I* am a straight A student, Mr. Campbell, which is why I'm calling for help. I'd like to keep it that way. I don't have time to flirt anyway. I have life goals too, Mr. Nose-Up-In-The-Air.'"

I snorted. "I'll bet that put him in his place." Totally. Like the little Jack Russel terrier at the edge of town when he's yapping at the cows across the fence. *Take that, you beast.*

"Well, he did agree to help me, so it worked." She grinned. "And then we met… Oh my word. I did not know science nerds were available in that style." Pausing, she cocked her head. "Have you met my husband?"

"No, not that I know of."

She sighed. I could actually visualize tiny, glowing hearts dancing around her head. "Turned you to mush, huh?"

She sat up straighter. "I wouldn't say that."

"Have you seen your face when you talk about him?"

Her cheeks flushed pink, and she swished a hand at me. "Oh, come on now. You know how it is."

I cocked an eyebrow. "Uh, actually. No. Single, remember? Surely you didn't forget that—everyone else in town is keenly aware of it."

"Oh yeah?" Leaning forward, she lifted a mischievous brow. "Any good setups?"

"Really?"

"Oh come on. Tell. You must."

Groaning, I rolled my eyes. "Mrs. Anderson—you know, our secretary?—insisted I meet her thirty-five-year-old son when he came home for Thanksgiving. He was normal looking, I guess, but he must have doused himself in whatever fragrance he was wearing and spent half the thirty minutes we met for coffee checking his phone. The other half he spent telling me how glad he was that he left this homespun town and how he couldn't understand why a young woman like me would have signed up to live here on purpose. Then he looked at me point blank and asked, "Do you have a criminal history? Or maybe you're running. Is that it?"

Anastacia curled against the cushions, laugher shaking her whole body.

"So that was a real winner." I rolled my eyes and shook my head. "Then Mrs. Blake at church thought that her great-nephew would be such a catch, and—this is a quote—'he's been saving himself for a nice girl like you.' End quote. Do you know how awkward that kind of a conversation is with a seventy-year-old woman? We're talking walk-into-school-in-your-underwear awkward. But what could I do? So I met him. He wore dress pants left over from the early nineties—they were wrinkled and covered in cat hair—and one of those crazy print sweaters from the same decade. First questions out of his mouth were, how many youngins was I willing to raise? And have I ever milked a goat?"

She actually had tears leaking from her eyes. "No. Way."

"Stone-cold serious, girlfriend. That ended the local setups for me. Apparently Mrs. Rustin has a nephew that used to come around who's supposed to be quite a looker—and normal—but he went off the grid. Just as well, because my version of normal and these ladies' version are not the same. If I was looking for romance, I'm not going to find it here. But that's okay. I wasn't really looking."

Anastacia wrangled down her giggles, shaking her head. "Come on now. You never know…"

I held up a hand. "Done. Next subject. How's about you tell me why your car was on fire? That sounds way more interesting."

She studied me with laughter still in her eyes, but also with a calm softness behind the giggles. "I like you, Kirstin Hill. I'm so glad we're friends. Moving here was hard, you know? Not knowing anyone and feeling like you're intruding into what has already been established. I was afraid I'd never find a place to fit."

"What?" My forehead scrunched. I could feel the pull of wrinkles. "You? Miss Happiness USA? Come on now…"

"For reals! I'd only ever lived in the small town where I grew up—except college, and that's not the same. I was scared to death to be the outsider, and I actually cried a little when Joe White convinced Mitch that he should set up practice here."

For the first time since I met this woman, her grin faded.

"Not only was it not home, but he'd be opening a clinic on his own in a town that didn't really have much for medical services. How lonely was that going to be?"

Yeah. That would be hard. "Wow, how's it working out?"

She shrugged, the light in her eyes dimming just a bit. "He's busy. Really busy. But we knew that would happen." Sitting straighter, she smiled again—and somehow it looked genuine. "But now look! I have a friend. And we can hang out, right?"

I mirrored her joy. "Yeah. Definitely."

A yawn pulled on her mouth, and I checked out the massive clock on the long, shiplap-covered wall behind us. Ten twenty-seven. One look back at Anastacia told me Mitch hadn't been exaggerating. The woman was done.

"Looks like your carriage has turned to a pumpkin, Cinderella."

She yawned again. "Huh?"

"You're done, girlie." I smiled. "So I'll scoot. But I want to hear the car fire story tomorrow."

A sleepy smile smoothed over her mouth. "Okay. Meet at the Sweet Tooth?"

"Sure. Ten?"

"You bet."

I found my way to the door and pulled it open. Anastacia had followed me, so when I turned, she was only two steps behind.

"I'm glad too," I said. "About the friend thing. Fitting into a small town is harder than I thought. I was kind of afraid I never would because I'm a city girl."

Anastacia shrugged. "My mom always said a little friendliness goes a long way. Guess she was right."

I nodded, turning toward the steps that would take me to the sidewalk that would lead me to my car parked on the street. "Good night, Miss Happiness. I'll catch you tomorrow."

"Good night, City Girl."

My breath came out in little white puffs that glowed under the streetlights. Above me, the clear sky sang *hallelujah* while the moon grinned, as if God had told them to just for me.

That was a lovely thought.

A little friendliness goes a long way…

Another lovely thought. I wondered why I hadn't approached this move with it in the first place. Maybe it'd be easier to find a way to be a part of the community I was falling in love with if I showed the people in it that I *wanted* to be part of it.

Seemed like a good plan. Now, if only I could come up with one to solve the Cupcake Dilemma as well.

Maybe Anastacia could help.

Chapter 5

Everything about the Sweet Tooth Bakery is charming. And honestly, maybe a touch feminine, which is why you could understand my initial shock at meeting the owner/baker Ian Connealy.

I know. You've been wondering when that guy was going to come back in.

Let me tell you though. I didn't figure him into this story. I was completely good with me, my classroom of second graders, and my new friend Anastacia, the perfectly perky model soon-to-be mama.

I like things simple. Complicated was why I left the city. It was too much of everything. Congestion. Population. Complication. I wanted the simple life, and for the most part, I found it in Rock Creek. The charm of the small town was a side perk that I embraced, and part of that charm was this little bakery next to the coffee shop. The front retail side was fairly deep— enough for half a dozen round tables scattered across the wooden floor, each accompanied by four metal chairs upholstered in sparkly blue vinyl, giving an immediate retro vibe.

The counter was high, accommodating the pastry display case full of Ian's specialties: monster-man cookies and *I think I need bigger pants* cupcakes. Behind the counter, suspended on the wall space separating the retail store from the kitchen, a span of chalkboard listed the day's specials and prices, and of course *The Sweet Tooth* was written with pink and blue chalk in large loopy letters.

Unlike some shops, whose goods looked better than they actually were, the Sweet Tooth delivered as promised. Those cupcakes were amazing, and it was highly possible that if I spent too much time in that place, I would definitely need bigger pants. And it would be worth it.

Anastacia met me as planned, two steaming cups of coffee filling her hands. Had this been my first time in the Sweet Tooth, I would have worried that the owner would be offended by the fact that we were bringing in drinks from another shop, but I'd since learned that Ian and Ms. Ruthie, the coffee shop owner, had an understanding—and a cute working relationship that toed a flirty edge, except it wasn't, because she could be his grandmother. I'd also discovered that Ian Connealy was virtually unoffendable.

That had been an interesting find. Two months before, one of my students had burst through the baker's front door while I was enjoying one of my favorites—the Rocky Road Toad—and the boy's dad bellowed into the back kitchen when Ian didn't immediately appear. "Hey, Baker Boy. Get up here."

Ian had sauntered from the kitchen, a big old grin spread wide on his face. "What's happening, Tom?"

"I'm starving, but don't you dare tell Dre I brought Keegan in here for lunch."

Tipping his head, Ian raised an eyebrow. "Don't want her to know how unhealthy you are?"

"No, she's already aware of that situation." Tom grinned. "We packed a real lunch, by the way. Dre doesn't need to know that I'm addicted to your girly sugar cakes."

"Well, if you bought her one, I can put it in a to-go box, and you'd be totally legit."

Keegan Kent, the seven-year-old, grinned and shook his head. "He's done that too much already, right, Dad? Mom's gonna catch on."

Ian laughed, slid the pastry display box open from the back side, and reached for a Peanut Butter Boss. "This is the one, right?" he asked Tom, not waiting for an answer. "And you, little man, what's it gonna be today?"

Keegan pulled his lips and eyebrows together in a hard *I'm a thinking* look. Big deal, getting cupcakes. Didn't wanna miff that. "What's in a Razzle-Dazzle Toothache?"

"Sugar." Ian winked. "It's a birthday cake flavor with sprinkles baked in and a buttercream frosting."

"Is there frosting in the middle?"

"Of course. Want one?"

Keegan grinned, and Ian served. One eyebrow hitched up again, and he eyed Tom. "Dre's favorite is the Vanilla Buttercream Blast. In case you didn't know."

"You know how to work this deal, don't you?"

Ian spread his long arms and shrugged, mischief scrawled all over his good-humored face. "Gotta make a living."

"Think you're making a killing."

Ian chuckled.

"Box it up. Maybe I'll grab her one of those fancy lattes she gets, and..." Tom wiggled his eyebrows.

"You can just leave the rest of that thought in your head, Tom. Keegan and I don't want to know."

Tom laughed, paid, and he and Keegan moseyed out of the shop. I'd sat at a far corner table, amused by the whole exchange and kind of intrigued by the baker's easygoing manner. He seemed to know everyone in town. He seemed not to care if the guys came in calling him Baker Boy and his shop girly.

He also seemed like a total mystery. Mostly because he could use an oven.

I chuckled over that memory as Anastacia led me to the very same table I'd sat at the day I'd watched Tom and Keegan Kent.

"What's so funny?" she asked me, easing her round belly between the chair and the table.

"Just this place. What did you think when you first met the baker?"

"Are you kidding? I thought cupcakes and eye candy? Sign me up." She blushed and winked.

"That's hardly fair. You're gorgeous, pregnant, and already married. Leave some game for the rest of us."

Her eyebrows quirked. "Thought you weren't looking."

"Yeah, well…I'm not." I cleared my throat, pushed against the heat spreading over my chest, and quickly changed the subject. "So. Car fire. Go."

One adorable dimple poked into her cheek as the same corner of her mouth lifted. "We were on our honeymoon, driving through the mountains. He had this old sedan. Still drives it—because it's paid for and he's the responsible finance type." She winked. "Anyway, being the responsible type that he is, he'd checked the oil and other fluids before we set off on this cross-country trip we'd planned. So when we started having car trouble near the top of a pass, he was totally bemused. 'I checked everything,' he said. 'We should be good. This shouldn't be a problem.' In the meantime, smoke starts curling into the cab and oozing out from under the hood. So he pulls over, pops the hood, and a flame spurts out. Well, you can imagine we bailed out of the car pretty quick and ran to a safe distance, thinking the whole thing's going to explode. It didn't. In fact, the flame died back, and all we saw was smoke curling into the clear mountain air. So that's when I was like, 'It's fine, babe. It's all good—it's gonna work out.'"

I laughed. "And that's when he told you it wasn't fine, because the car was on fire?"

"Right." She rolled her eyes. "But guess what? It was fine. Turned out he'd left the rag on top of the oil cap, and it had caught on fire. Luckily, it burned itself out, and everything was fine. But oh my goodness, Mitch was pretty tied up about it." Chuckling, she shook her head. "Poor man. He worries about everything, and now he checks the engine before we go anywhere. It's borderline ridiculous."

Shaking my head, I smiled. "Gotta tell you here, Anastacia, that wasn't nearly as funny as the teaser you gave. I have way more dramatic kitchen catastrophes than that."

She nodded. "I know. That's why I stick to the headline and leave the rest." Leaning in, she winked. "But kitchen catastrophes? This I must hear."

"I don't know…"

"Come on. I told you the car fire story."

"I know, but that wasn't even your fault, and it flamed out right when it was getting interesting."

The screech of a chair being pulled out next to me interrupted our lighthearted debate. Ian tipped the chair onto one leg, spun it around until the back faced the table, and then dropped onto the seat backward, saddle-style. "Did I hear something about car fires and kitchen catastrophes?" His dark eyes held a smile—normal for him, as far as I could tell—as he glanced between the two of us.

"Oh yes." Anastacia's trademark wide smile met his grin. "But as Kirstin here was saying, the car fire is a dud. It's much better left at the intro, and now that you've heard the rest of the story, it won't be nearly as funny."

I shot him a sassy smirk. "That's what you get for eavesdropping."

"Oh." He grabbed his left shoulder, as if I'd wounded him. "Salty, eh? Here I am just trying to be a nice guy, coming over to see what the pretty ladies would like from the pastry box, and I get slammed for happening to overhear an interesting conversation."

He winked. It was kind of cute, and I laughed. "Okay, fine. You're excused, but only because you own the place."

"If I toss in a pair of free caramel rolls, do I get full forgiveness?"

Anastacia rubbed her hands together. "Now we're talking."

Nodding, Ian pushed up from the chair with both hands gripping the back and then paused where he stood. "On the condition, of course, that I get to hear the kitchen-disaster story."

Both sets of eyes landed on me, and they both arched their eyebrows while they waited for me to agree.

"Which one?" I mumbled.

Ian's head fell backward as he laughed. He buttoned a smile on me. "Excellent. Don't start before I get back."

A small cluster of customers passed through the front door as he pivoted to go back to the pastry shelf, the little bell over the door chiming a happy tune.

"Kale! Joe!" Ian paused just before he slipped behind the counter, squatting to greet Sydney White. "How's the Super Syd?"

"I'm awesome." Sydney was a first grader—not one of Anastacia's kids, but well known to almost everyone in the school. She had the gift of charm and sometimes used it mischievously, but was usually just flat-out adorable. Among the teachers at school, the rumor had her playing cupid for her mom and Joe White. I was new, so I hadn't witnessed the story unfold, but the bits and pieces I'd gathered were Hallmark-movie endearing, and knowing the little bit of Sydney that I did, I believed it.

"I can see you're awesome, and I hear you're crazy fast on the playground."

Sydney bit her lip and grinned, nodding. "Yeppers. No more limping around for this girl."

Ian held out a fist, and she bumped it with hers. "Glad to hear it, kid. Also glad to hear that you're going to be a big sister." He winked up toward Kale.

"I know. I'm going to be awesome at that."

"You know it."

"Okay, Sydney." Kale dropped her hand on the girl's dark-brown braid. "I think your head is big enough now."

Sydney pressed both hands against her temples and then scrunched a scowl. "It feels the same size to me, Momster."

Joe snorted a laugh, and Ian stood and slipped behind the counter. "Okay, what'll it be?"

Anastacia nudged me with a foot under the table. "Aren't they so cute?" she whispered.

"Totally." I leaned on an elbow, focusing my attention on her.

"And Ian…" She sat back and crossed her arms.

I exaggerated an eye roll.

"I checked both hands. No ring." She ended with a singsongy voice.

Still in drama mode, I dropped my head into my arm. "Not you too."

"He looks totally normal—actually, on the hot side of normal—and he seems really nice."

"He probably has a long-distance girlfriend somewhere waiting for him to get things settled here."

"What woman would let a man like that move into a small town looking all single and available without her?"

I stared at her. And blinked. "Don't you dare."

"I have the best idea."

"No."

"It's awesome."

I sat up. "I'm serious."

Her *Tangled* voice reemerged. "It'll be so fun."

"I've heard that before."

"Trust me—I know what I'm doing."

I felt my forehead pinch. "Is this one of those *the car is on fire but it's fine* kind of things?"

"All right, ladies." Ian strode back our way, a tray of two caramel rolls resting on one palm. "You'd better not be talking about disasters without me."

No. Anastacia was concocting one *with him*. I shot her a warning glance. She shrugged.

"What did I miss?" He looked from me to her and then back again.

"Nothing," I said. "I was just deciding which kitchen-fail story I'd be willing to tell you."

"How many have you had?"

"Can you count the stars?"

"That bad, huh?"

"You know how most people give dishes or flowers or decorations when someone they know and love moves? My mother gave me a fire extinguisher." I kept my voice flat, my face stoic.

Ian and Anastacia both laughed.

"What provoked that gift?" Anastacia asked.

"Uh…there's a list. How about you pick a kitchen scenario, and I'll tell you how I screwed it up."

"All right." Ian planted an elbow on the table and leaned against the palm of his hand. "Casseroles—the one-dish wonder. Go."

"Easy." I cocked an eyebrow, as if taking on a challenge I should be proud of. "When I was in high school, my mom put together a lasagna and stowed it in the fridge for us because she was going on a girls' weekend trip with some of her friends. She left detailed instructions for me and my sister, starting with *remove the plastic wrap that is under the foil and replace the foil overtop*."

"Well, that one's predictable." Ian sat up. "You forgot to remove the plastic, and it melted."

I sat back and crossed my arms. "It gets better."

"Yeah?" Anastacia leaned in. "Did you fix the melted plastic problem?"

"Well, I attempted to. I smelled the burning plastic while I was heating up the green beans on the stove top, and face-palmed myself. Panicked, I ripped open the oven and tried to remove the casserole dish before I put on gloves. Luckily, the burning sensation sank into my fingers before I had it completely out of the oven, so it sat there, balanced on the top rack—half on and half off, while I slapped the oven mitts onto my now-burned fingers. I pulled that sucker out, but my fingers still hurt, so I slid it onto the glass-top stove and flicked off the mitts while I scurried over to the sink. But then while I stood at the sink letting cold water run over my red fingertips, a sudden pop sounded from the oven. I jumped back just as the second, louder pop sounded and lasagna exploded everywhere."

Anastacia's mouth gaped, and Ian bent over the table, hand rubbing his neck.

"What happened?" she asked.

He shook his head. "You had the burner on the stove top on, didn't you?"

"Yeah." I shut my eyes and shook my head, still seeing the mess in my mother's kitchen. "I'd turned on the wrong burner, so the green beans were sitting on a cold burner doing nothing, while the glass casserole dish was sitting on the hot burner that I'd actually turned on. It was such a mess."

"Oh no!" Anastacia's smile was still in place, but genuine sympathy rang through her voice. "But really, that was just a series of unfortunate mistakes. Not entirely your fault."

"Yeah, my kitchen life could be a Lemony Snicket book."

Chuckling, Ian leaned toward me. "Were your fingers okay?"

"Yeah, and I didn't even get hit with casserole dish shrapnel. Only my mom's kitchen suffered any damage. We were finding lasagna sauce in very strange places for months."

"Well…" Anastacia leaned in again. "I still think that was just bad luck. If that's the worst—"

I held up a hand. "It's not. But that's okay. I've come to terms with it. I cannot kitchen. It's my lot in life."

Both chuckled at my overdramatization. With a hand on his thigh, Ian tipped my direction. "I'll bet that you just need a success to change your trajectory."

"What?"

"Oh!" Anastacia squealed, clapping her hands. "Yes, I have the best idea!"

I eyed her, remembering those very same words coming from her, sans Ian, just a few minutes before.

She wiggled her brows.

I shook my head.

She rubbed her palms together. And plunged. "Kirstin was assigned desserts for the Valentine's Day barn dance."

I cleared my throat. "We're not talking about that right now."

An eyebrow arched over Ian's right eye. "What's this?"

"Sure we are." She clapped again. "Ian makes the best cupcakes."

True. Maybe she wasn't setting me up here. I relaxed.

"Aha." He leaned backward in his chair, his unringed fingers clasping the back again. "You want me to do your work for you." A look of mock indignation lifted his brow into his backward ball cap.

"Well, no." I sputtered, blushing. "I'd buy them from you, of course. Just a business deal."

Anastacia grinned her winning, *everything is fine, better than fine* grin. Ian smirked. I wondered why placing an order for cupcakes had turned into an amusing hold-my-breath-and-wait-for-his-answer kind of moment. What on earth...

"Nope."

My mouth fell open, and I stared at him. "What?"

"Not gonna do it."

"Are you kidding? I'm placing an order here for like two hundred cupcakes!"

"I told you—you just need one success."

"I told you I blew up a lasagna."

He shrugged. "You just need taught."

"I'm not that interested."

He crossed his arms and grinned. "Then no cupcakes for you."

"Wait." Anastacia stepped in again. "Are you saying you'll teach her? You'll help her make the two hundred cupcakes?"

Ian nodded, drummed on the table, and then stood. "Take it or leave it."

I stared at him. More.

"You can let me know what you decide before you leave." He winked and then turned back for the kitchen.

I blinked and turned my dumbfounded look on Anastacia. "What just happened?"

"I think he wants to teach you how to bake."

"That is a terrible idea."

"No, it's not. It's fine. It's all good. Everything is going to work out. You'll see."

Visions of fire spurting out of my oven, and microwave, and from a pot on top of the stove—all of them events that actually had happened—played through my mind.

"I think you're being delusional again."

Anastacia only laughed, and the Cupcake Dilemma took on a whole new twist.

Chapter 6

Monday's spelling list included the words *cute, cookies, correct,* and for bonus points, *unicorn.* While my second graders were busy practicing word usage by creating sentences with their word lists, I made up my own sample sentences.

This afternoon Ms. Hill will learn the <u>correct</u> way to bake <u>cookies</u> with the <u>cute</u> baker. And <u>unicorns</u> will appear on Main Street.

I felt sweaty in my teal super-soft cardigan and hoped that my nylon-and-lace flowy top underneath the open sweater didn't have pit marks. What in the world was Ian Connealy thinking? Clearly he hadn't understood the depth of my kitchen ineptness. He was a baker—in his business, surely taking on a large order of cupcakes was a good idea.

"Ms. Hill?" Keegan Kent waved at me, the tone of his voice letting me know that this hadn't been the first time he'd tried to get my attention. I snapped from my dazed stare at the Smartboard up front, where the word list glowed on the LED screen.

"Yes, Keegan? Do you need help?"

"You were staring," he said, one ornery eyebrow raised.

"I was just thinking about something I have to do later."

"Must be something hard. Your forehead was kind of mushed up."

"Thank you, Keegan. Did you have a question?"

"No. Just wondered if you were okay."

He smiled—it looked like a Dennis the Menace grin, all mischievous and cute at the same time. Kind of like Ian's grin when I'd skulked up to the cash register, where he was wiping down the counter, just before Anastacia and I had left Saturday morning.

"Okay, you have a deal," I'd mumbled, looking at Ian like he was in for it. Because he was.

Cue the cute troublemaker grin. "Excellent. We'll start on Monday afternoon."

My right eyebrow rocketed toward my hairline. "We will?"

"Of course. One must practice." He continued working, as if this were a normal conversation.

"When did you think we'd have time to practice?"

He stopped, his chin tilted while his face radiated little-boy mischief. "I just told you. Monday afternoon, whenever you get done with school. And then Tuesday. After that, Wednesday."

I braced my hands on my hips. "How do you know I work at the school?"

His eyes rolled as if *I* were the crazy one. "Ms. Kirstin Hill. Second-grade teacher. Likes the Rocky Road Toads, Red Velvet Delights, and occasionally will go for the Dark and Dangerous. But I think that's only for a bad day. Keegan Kent is one of your students, and here's a bit that maybe you don't know, but you might need to." He leaned across the counter and dropped his voice to a whisper. "Pretty sure the kid's got a crush on his teacher."

All of that ended with a wink, and then Ian crossed his arms and rocked back on his heels—a silent sign that he thought I should be impressed.

I blinked twice and stared at him for two more breaths after that. "Are you a stalker?"

Laughter shook his shoulders. "Nope. Just a guy running a business in a small town. And since you're the new teacher, you get noticed."

I crossed my arms. "Anastacia's a new teacher too."

"Right. Married to Mitch Campbell, the new and only doctor in town. Likes the Carmel Fudge Smudge, and Mitch goes for the Simple Spice. She's a coffee drinker, but I'm pretty sure he only ever drinks water. They're complete opposites, but it works for them. Anything else you want to know?"

I fought against the amusement tickling my mouth. The smile pushed its way out anyway, and I shook my head. "What time again on Monday?"

"Whenever you get here. I close at six, but we can work after that if we need to."

I turned to go but stopped two steps toward the exit, glancing over my shoulder at him again. "You might regret this."

"I doubt it."

"You could call my mother—she'd corroborate my story."

"I'm not scared."

"Hope you're insured."

He'd laughed, and I'd left with a burned-in impression of the smile that resembled Keegan Kent's.

Recovering back to the present, I glanced over at Keegan again. He sat with his shoulders bent over the desk, scrawling out his sentences with that yellow number 2 pencil. After a moment, he glanced back at me and grinned when he found me watching. Both eyebrows wiggled up and down, and he waved.

I barely held in a snort-laugh. The little rascal was cute, and he knew it. Pretty sure Ian had been just like him at age eight.

A quick glance at the clock told me it was 2:52. Thirty-eight more minutes and I'd dismiss the kids. Another hour's worth of work waited for me at my desk, and then...

I'd find out how much Ian was like eight-year-old Keegan. And he'd find out how kitchen inept I really was.

Heh-heh-heh. The gleeful chuckle floated through my mind. I was ready. Pretty sure Ian was not.

***

"My new student."

Ian's call met me as I stepped past the clinking bell of the front door.

"Just in time to help with the predinner rush."

I glanced around the store, beating back the heat climbing onto my face as I met the smiles of several people I didn't yet know.

Hands pressed to the countertop, Ian stood next to the pastry case and beside the cash register, with a look of humored delight. "Change your mind?"

I walked toward him. "Is that an option?"

"Not if you want cupcakes from the Sweet Tooth."

I neared the front counter, and he cocked his head in a *come on* gesture, indicating the door that led into the back kitchen.

Following him, I rubbed my hands together. "I really think you're going to regret this."

Ignoring my comment, he pointed to a door on my right as we entered his industrial kitchen. "That's my office. You can toss your coat in there. There's an extra apron hanging on one of the hooks near the door. Grab one. And a hair net from the box on my desk."

"Hair net?"

"Yeah. Because no one wants to find strands of your spice-cake-colored hair in their cupcakes. Plus, it's the rules. You must comply."

Eyeing his ball-capped head, I twisted my mouth to one side. "And your hat satisfies those rules—or are they more like guidelines?" I mocked a Captain Barbosa accent.

He molded an imitation of what he must have thought was a stern teacher mask and pinched at the black hairline peeking out from his backward-turned hat. The webbing of a net stretched forward, caught between his thumb and index finger. "Compliant. See?"

Sighing, I let my head drop backward dramatically. "Great. Not only will you witness the disaster of Kirstin meets kitchen, I'll be modeling a cafeteria-lady style while we whip up disaster."

"You can borrow a hat to wear over the net, if it'd make you feel better."

I landed a sassy look on him, and he just kept right on grinning. Like Keegan. So I sauntered toward his office, working pretty hard at looking grumpy about this whole deal. That was *not* working, because Ian was just an all-out goofball, and I couldn't help but feel happy to be there, even if I sensed the imminent humiliation about to crash down around me.

His office was tidy. Minimal furniture—a desk, a lamp, a swivel chair that sat to the side of where it was supposed to be, and a rack of hooks on the wall opposite the desk. Hanging my coat on a peg, I noted there wasn't a coat for him anywhere in sight. It was the end of January, and there was four inches of snow outside, so that made me question his sanity. More.

There was an apron on the end peg closest to the door, just as he'd promised. After snatching it, I ducked into the head loop and fumbled around with the ties at my back. Ian's chuckle floated from the doorway, and then he was behind me, removing my clumsy fingers from the tie straps.

"They're extra long on purpose." He tugged the two into what felt like an X and then spun me around to face him, one arm arced over my head as if we were twirling on a dance floor. Before I inhaled the next breath, his hands were at my middle, looping the tie ends into a bow. "See? Next time you can do it yourself."

I glanced down—his hands were in his own space now, and he'd taken a step back—and then I glanced up. "Was that lesson number one?"

"Sure. Number two…"

He turned, snatched a wad of gauzy netting from the Kleenex-like box on his desk, and stepped back into my space. Somehow he managed to pinch the little wad of whatever that thing was made of in between his middle and ring fingers while at the same time turning me back around and gathering my long hair into a loose mess at my neck.

"Do you fix girls' hair often?"

"I used to pull my sister's. Does that count?"

I reached back and rescued my mane. "In that case, hands off." With a quick flip, pull, and one last tug, I fixed a messy bun with the tie I usually kept at the ready on my wrist.

"Impressive." His hands came over my head, near my nose, and then the rascal hooked one end of the net just above my upper lip and stretched it over my scalp, letting it go when he got to the hairline at my neck.

Turning, I lifted my brows and tilted my chin up. "Perfect. Now I'm ready to head down the street toward the bank, right?"

"It's a good look."

"Thanks?" I pinched the end that had snagged on the tip of my nose and moved it up to my hairline. "I think I'd see better with it like this though."

"Fair enough. One last touch." He leaned past me, grabbed a ball cap from a peg, and dropped it backward on top of my head.

I adjusted it so that it wasn't hanging over one eye. "Acceptable?"

He mashed his lips together, tilted his head as if my question required a real inspection, and then shrugged. "I'll take you."

"Oh good," I deadpanned. "I was nervous."

I caught his boyish smile as he turned away and stepped back through the door and into the kitchen. Following him, I took in the lay of the land. *My next victim…heh-heh-heh.* The biggest oven I'd ever seen took center stage on the far wall, and the stainless-steel countertop L-ed from it into the back wall on my right. It stretched another five feet before it dead-ended into a set of stacked ovens.

"I could do quite the significant damage with this kind of equipment." I stopped in the middle of the wide space, turning slowly. A giant industrial freestanding mixer sat to the left of the oven. Two other KitchenAid mixers posted up on the far ends of a six-foot stainless-steel island that stretched between the back wall and the door to the retail part of his bakery.

"Imagine the batter flying. The smoke curling from every gleaming oven." I set a wicked grin on him and rubbed my palms together. "You have no idea what you've done."

He lifted his eyebrows. "I'm watching you, Ms. Hill. There'll be no bakery mischief in my kitchen."

"No promises."

Ian rolled his eyes. "All right, be serious now. Tell me what you know."

"My food comes from a microwave."

"All of it?"

"Unless it comes out of someone else's kitchen or a drive-through, then pretty much, yes. All of it."

"That's just wrong."

"No, it's safer that way. I keep telling you…"

"One success." He held up an index finger and then tapped it on my nose. "It's gonna turn it all around for you. So we'll start with something easy."

"Easy is relative. You do know that, don't you?"

"Cookies. I've got a fail-safe Monster Cookie recipe."

He really wasn't getting this. I shrugged. "Okay. Where do we start?"

With a hand on my elbow, he guided me to a KitchenAid and waved at a sheet of paper tucked into protective plastic. "Read through all the directions first. Supplies are labeled." He bent and pointed at the giant containers on the shelf below the counter. "I'll be back in a few minutes to check on you."

Two pats on my back, and he strode around the island and toward the door.

"This is a really bad idea," I called out to him.

He turned, flashing a smile as he pushed against the door to the storefront with his backside. "You've got this."

What in the ever? Lifting my eyebrows, I scowled at the door as it smacked its way closed on its hinges. Ian just went from goofy to weird. Why was he even doing this? I just wanted the dang cupcakes for the dance!

Maybe he needed an employee but couldn't afford to hire someone?

The sneaky Pete.

No, that couldn't be right. He wouldn't drag in a self-proclaimed kitchen-fail if he actually needed help. People like me created more *work*—they didn't *help*.

Perhaps a desperately lonely man?

Gooey chocolate eyes, an eternal grin, and features that made him look like a much-happier version of Bruce Wayne—the Christian Bale variety? Yeah, probably not.

Whatever. I was there. Might as well whip something up. I scanned through the recipe—the ingredients list, followed by instructions. Measure, weigh (weigh? Didn't even understand that…so I mentally skipped it), pour, mix…and ta-da! Cookies.

Couldn't be that hard, could it? The instructions weren't that complicated. I was in an equipped kitchen; all ingredients were present. I was going to do this.

I imagined calling my mom. She'd freak!

Mom*: Cookies, Kirstin? Like homemade, from scratch, and you mixed them up and baked them? Honey! You're so grown up. And also…tell me about this baker…*

Me: *He's weird, Mom. In a funny, keeps-me-snorting, and sometimes belly-laughing, strangely-happy-guy kind of way. I think you'd like him.*

Mom: *So…*

I rolled my eyes, closing off that imaginary conversation. Who was weird?

By the time I clicked on sane Kirstin thoughts, I'd pulled out all of the required ingredients from the bottom shelf and from the refrigerator and lined them up in no particular order on the counter next to my assigned mixer. Let the concocting begin.

Flour, sugar, salt, baking soda, butter, milk, vanilla, peanut butter, oats, chocolate chips, and candy-covered chocolates. There was a handwritten star under the printed-out list of ingredients. *Add extra tsp of vanilla.*

Huh. A secret ingredient. Wonder if he'd pay me to keep quiet?

My confidence fluttered as I measured and dumped the ingredients in the order that I'd set them up on the counter. Poised to pour the required vanilla into the bowl, I glanced up at the click of the hinges on the door across the room.

Ian smacked his hands together once and continued my direction. "How's it go—" He stopped as he peered into my mixing bowl and then peeked at me from his bent-head position. "Did you read the directions?"

"Yep."

"I don't think so."

I scowled. "What are you talking about? What's missing?"

"You're just dumping stuff in there."

"Okay…" I gave him a toothy, innocent sort of smile.

"There's an order to this chaos. You have to mix up the dry ingredients separately. And you need to cream the butter, peanut butter, and eggs before you go adding flour to them."

I mirrored his tipped position to look into the mixing bowl. "I told you this was a bad idea."

He stood straight and reached for a giant spoon that was hanging on an S hook on the wall. "No big deal. It's fixable."

"Ian, you have a business to run, and it's an hour before closing. Wouldn't it be better—"

"If you go work the front? Yes. Good idea. We'll finish this after everyone leaves." He finished scooping the ingredients I was supposed to "cream" first out of the mixing bowl.

I stood there, lifted eyebrows, watching him. He stopped and looked up, and when his eyes connected with mine, I might have held my breath.

Not because of that. Don't go making assumptions. I was holding my breath because...

Okay, fine. He was cute. Hot, even. And for a moment, he stared at me. You'd hold your breath too.

"Simon says go." He grinned.

"Huh?"

"You looked like you were waiting for more. Like Simon Says. So..."

I rolled my eyes. "Got it. I'll work the front. You can finish the cookies."

"No. We'll finish the cookies together. I've got to grab some more Peanut Butter Bombs, and then I'll be out front too."

He winked and then turned, and I was left standing next to the island.

Simon said go. So I went. We worked together—which was actually pretty fun. His closing rush was impressive—but he didn't fail to address each customer by name, ask how their test or pet or mother-in-law was, and say he'd see them on whatever that person's regular day was. Yeah, he knew that too.

Handsome and kind. What exactly was the reason for this man's singleness?

One of two questions that poked around in my mind while we wiped down the counter and tabletops after he'd locked the door. I was only willing to ask one—and it wasn't going to be that one—but I waited until we were back in the kitchen, whipping up some Monster Cookies.

"How is it you missed learning how to make cookies?" Ian asked as we scooped the last of the gooey temptation into balls and placed them neatly on a parchment-lined tray.

I shrugged. "I…was never really interested, I guess. Mom was busy—it was just her and me and my sister; she and my dad split up when I was twelve—and I had a tendency to make a mess in the kitchen, so we just skipped that part of growing up, I guess." I cocked an eyebrow as I looked back at him. "Maybe the real question in this scenario is, how is it you became a baker?"

His grin slid into the kind that softens faces when there was a happy memory behind it. "My mom." He looked me in the eye before he continued. "I always had to work twice as hard for the good grades that seemed to come pretty easy to my brother—but I did it, because I'm competitive. My mom though. She always seemed to know when I was on the edge of my threshold for books, and she'd say, 'Ian, you need a brain break. Let's go make something amazing.' And we did. We'd look up a recipe, make sure we had everything we needed, and then whip up something delicious. Fast-forward about fifteen years. I was working as a financial planner, hating it—the pressure and the stress and just trying to be someone that I'm really not, and I found myself baking during the evenings and weekends. When my brother got married and his bride asked me to do cupcakes for their wedding, something clicked." He tapped the side of his head. "So I used the degree I studied for, worked in the financial world for a couple more years, saving and planning, and then moved out here." He spread his arms wide. "Now I have this."

"And it makes you happy."

"Well, I wasn't unhappy with life, just my career choice, but yeah, I love what I'm doing, and I love Rock Creek, so double bonus, right?"

"Wait—you're not from Rock Creek?"

"Nope. Only been here for three years. A college buddy, Jeff, he was from this small town, and we kept in touch. He'd say every now and then, 'You should try the small-town life, buddy.' So when I decided to try for my own bakery, I looked it up, checked out the real estate, which was really affordable, and found this building for sale. It was in rough shape, but it gave me the chance to renovate the way I wanted, and so far, it's worked out pretty well."

"Huh." I leaned against the wall on the other side of the island. "I would have sworn you were born here. You know everyone and fit in so well."

He tilted his head, studied me for a minute, and then opened his mouth to say something. But just as the words became sound, whatever he was going to say cut off as he jerked himself straight and sniffed. "What—" Another sniff, and then he whirled around to face the giant oven.

Pushing off the wall, I leaned over the counter so that I could see the oven too, and caught the flicker of a flame burst just as Ian yelled, "Fire!"

Yep. Right there in the oven.

I snatched the extinguisher he'd pointed out to me earlier. He went to the sink, grabbing a pan on the way. I beat him to the flames, ripped open the oven door, and pulled the trigger on the extinguisher. White foam spurted everywhere.

Once the flames were smothered, I looked up. Ian stood like a statue at the sink, the pan he'd filled with water poised for action and his mouth gaping.

Guess now he knew what he was dealing with. Figured the deal was off.

Chapter 7

"I think I've discovered our culprit." With oven mitts on, Ian slushed through the mess of white foamy fire-smothering gunk and pulled out the ashen remains of…

A towel.

I groaned, head-butting the cabinet to my right. "You've got to be kidding me."

"Look familiar?"

"Not anymore. I must have accidentally grabbed it when I picked up the cookie sheet." I stood up straighter. "I swear, Ian, I didn't mean to."

He studied me as if I were a puzzle, and then his natural grin surfaced again. "So this is your life, huh?"

My head dropped back as I shut my eyes. "Yeah, pretty much." I straightened and then pasted on a toothy *I'm sorry* grin. "I did warn you. Remember?"

He nodded. "You did."

"You didn't believe me."

He lifted his left shoulder and turned to dump the flame-broiled towel into the large garbage can near the sink. "It's just bad luck. That's all. Could happen to anyone." He flicked the oven mitts into the trash too— both now covered with white foam. "You were pretty quick on the draw with that fire extinguisher."

"I've had practice."

"See? Practice makes perfect."

I tipped my head and looked at him like he was nuts. Because I was pretty sure he was. "You're not—"

"Oh no. This ain't over, lady." Water splashed into the sink as he turned to wash his hands. "We're not done, and you're not quitting." He snatched a towel from the open shelf at eye level and then turned back to me. "However, you're going to have to help me out with dinner tonight."

"Dinner?" I felt one eyebrow pushing up into my forehead. "Sure. I guess I owe you dinner. Ms. May's Diner?"

"What? No. You're not *buying* me dinner. That's not what I meant."

"What did you mean then?"

"Well, I was telling you I bought this place as a renovation project, right?"

I waited, not following his bunny trail.

"I live in the loft above the bakery."

"Okay…"

"I didn't put in a kitchen."

"Wait—you don't have a kitchen?"

"That's what I'm telling you."

"You're a baker. How do you *not* have a kitchen?"

His arms spread out, palms up. "*This* is my kitchen. Didn't see a need to put one upstairs too. Especially since I'm working with a budget here."

I stared hard at him. "Even *I* have a kitchen."

"Good. We'll use that then."

"I thought all places had kitchens."

"What are you up for?"

My look pinched, and I tipped my head. Had he just ignored my last comment?

"I'm starving," he continued, "so I vote for something quick and easy. Like…"

"Are we talking about *cooking* dinner?"

"Yes. Thanks for catching up. We should decide what we're going to make before we leave, just in case you think we'll need to grab stuff at the store…"

"I don't even know if my oven works."

That seemed to distract him from his *let's make dinner* mission. "You don't know?"

"No, I've never turned it on."

He scowled. "That's weird."

I looked from him to the still-smoking, covered-in-white-stuff oven and back again, and then lifted the extinguisher, which was still in my hands. "Fire hazard. I stick with the microwave."

"You can't eat your meals from a microwave every day."

"Sure I can. I'm surviving just fine."

Shaking his head, he stepped toward his office, slipping his apron off as he moved. "That should not happen. I'm staging an intervention." He spun around to meet me as I followed his trail, one finger pointing up. "Tonight, we cook. We'll do classic and easy. Spaghetti. Get your things."

A chuckle pushed its way through my chest as I lifted off my apron. "You are a very strange bird."

"We all have our quirks." He stopped beside me, taking the apron from my hands and handing me my coat, which he'd retrieved from its peg. "And be nice. You just set fire to my kitchen."

"Okay, yeah. I'll clean it up as soon as everything cools down. I've had experience with that too. Hot soapy water works pretty well."

He waved me off as if it were no big deal. "It'll keep until after we eat." Two long strides took him out of his office, and I watched him as he continued toward the back door. He stopped, one hand on the knob, ready to push it open. "Coming?"

I looked back at the oven.

"It's fine, Kirstin. Truly. The smoke will clear, and we'll clean it up. After we eat—I'm hungry."

My focus zeroed in on him again. He smiled—the Keegan Kent kind of smile.

Who could say no to that?

***

Shopping with Ian was an entertaining, if not mildly embarrassing, experience.

I am the grab-something-quick-and-get-out-of-there sort. The hit-and-run grocery girl. This was not an approved approach for Ian Connealy.

"Hi, Mrs. Blake!" He stopped before we even made it through the sliding doors. "How's that nephew of yours keeping?"

"Oh, you know how he is." The old woman patted Ian's arm. "Likes to keep to himself out there on the old spread. But he comes in for coffee every now and then."

She eyed me, a hopeful gleam flashing through her expression—likely remembering when he came in to have coffee with me. When she looked back up to Ian, the flicker of whatever she'd thought faded. Stepping back, she seemed to take us both in, and then she nodded, her smile genuine, if not a little bit reserved.

"How are you, Ms. Hill?"

"I'm good," I stammered. "Yeah, just doing…good."

Ian stepped forward. "Can I help you get your groceries to the car?"

She shooed at him with her free hand. "I'm old, young man, but I'm still breathing. You go on now. Go make that pretty girl you've got with you laugh with your antics."

I watched for color to creep into his cheeks, because I could feel the heat on mine. It didn't. Ian just nodded, kept on grinning, and lifted a wave as he headed into the store.

"Looks like she knows you well enough," I said, keeping my stride to match his meander. "Antics. Sure you didn't grow up here?"

"Nah. But almost everyone comes into the Sweet Tooth sometime or another. They get to know me then. I'm pretty much all goofy all the time and can't seem to tame it."

We continued strolling toward the pasta aisle, Ian with his hands in his coat pockets, alert, and looking like he was ready for the next conversation with whomever wished one. I tugged on the lapels of my wool dress coat, wondering if I should worry about how this joint shopping trip would look to one of my students or their parents.

"What are you chewing on?" Ian turned into the aisle, glancing down at me.

"Chewing? Nothing."

"You're worrying about something. You have that Dark and Dangerous day kind of look on your face."

"You can tell what I'm going to order by my expression?"

"Only on Dark and Dangerous days."

"What do I look like?"

He stopped midway down the aisle, tipped his head, and then lifted his hand, palm toward his face, over his eyes. Slowly he lowered the screen he'd made, and his expression became a forced scowl.

I crossed my arms.

His mouth pulled down further.

I rolled my eyes. "Come on. It can't be that bad."

Probably, though, it could. I usually only ordered the Dark and Dangerous cupcake on days when life felt like a long run of *I don't know what the heck I'm doing, and I'm supposed to be an adult*. You know, those days when everything mocks your attempts at being put together and you figure that tomorrow you should just stay in bed? Those are Dark and Dangerous cupcake days.

For example, my parent-teacher conferences. It was a long day—like eleven full hours at work. And I have one student who I'm pretty sure is determined to be the death of me. He will not cooperate at all. Refuses to do his work. Screams when he's frustrated. And has thrown his pencil bag at me when I've tried to prompt him to get going.

He is failing second grade.

But that conference… It was worse than any day I'd had with him in the classroom. I was told under no circumstances could he fail. Nor could I push him to do his work. Nor was any form of discipline—removal of recess, detention, loss of privileges—acceptable. He was to pass. That was all.

I don't want him to fail. But just…pass him? How was that going to make him successful in life?

I was defeated by that one meeting, and the rest of the day, and all of the good conferences I'd had in it, seemed to fade to gray after that twenty-minute encounter.

It had been a Dark and Dangerous kind of evening.

Or, the day after I met with Mrs. Blake's son for coffee. Ugh. Another Dark and Dangerous kind of day.

Or the day I blew up my great-grandmother's teacups. Only I didn't go into the Sweet Tooth after that—I couldn't handle looking at Ian's perfectly made and frosted cupcakes with the harsh smell of my failure still clinging to my skin. But if I had, that would have been a Dark and Dangerous kind of day.

"Hey." Ian's hand warmed my shoulder, and he shook me. "Still with me?"

His exaggerated frown had vanished, and his dark eyes searched my face.

"Sure," I said, shrugging.

For two more breaths he studied me, and then he turned to the pasta on his left and lifted a box. "Traditional long, stringy noodles?" He fingered another box. "Or elbows?" Tucking that box into his arm, he made yet another selection. "Or penne?"

"Are we still talking about pasta here?"

"Pick one."

"I don't know the difference."

"Okay, just snatch one out of the air then, and that'll be what we go with."

"What?"

Before I breathed the question out, he had the boxes moving through the air. Juggling. The man was juggling pasta in the middle of the store.

"What are you doing?"

"Pick one. Do it quick before I mess up and one of these falls on the floor."

We ended up with the traditional long, stringy noodles—but I didn't snatch it cleanly from his act. The box slammed into my outstretched palm, bounced, because I can't catch, and then clattered to the floor. Luckily, the box didn't burst open, and I rescued it quick, before a store worker could catch us.

Ian snorted, and I giggled. After I had the box, I tugged on his elbow, dragging him down the aisle. "Just get whatever else you need for this crazy idea, and do it like a normal person, or you're going to get us kicked out."

"Me?" He pretended to drag behind me. "They wouldn't kick me out. I order in bulk from Tara. She loves me."

"I'm sure everyone in Rock Creek loves you."

That little-boy Keegan-ish smile met me when I glanced back.

He complied, finding the ingredients he thought we needed. A whole basketful of stuff later (I would have grabbed canned sauce. He had a whole bunch of other stuff he claimed would turn into sauce when he was done with it) and we were stepping out of the store, still laughing.

Chapter 8

I drove, and Ian rode with me, because I'd insisted I was coming back to the bakery after dinner to help him clean up. It was dark when we got to my house, and I scurried around, turning on lights and bumping up my thermostat while he unloaded the two grocery bags and a large stock pot from the bakery. He commented on my home—something about being cozy—and then started filling the pot with water. I excused myself to change out of my work clothes and wash my hands, only mildly self-conscious about him being in my house.

It wasn't a date. So nothing to feel self-conscious about. Ian was like this big, goofy teddy-bear friend. I kind of liked that. A lot. Plus, I could go put on my sweats and not feel the least bit worried about what he thought.

When I came out of my room, comfy clothes on and hair tied back, I found Ian in my living room, studying the art I had framed on the wall. He turned when he heard me behind him.

"Who did these?" His index finger grazed one of the four colored frames—hung in rainbow order—on my wall.

"They're mine."

His eyes lit, and he turned back to them. Each frame held one of my favorite pieces—the images whimsical and bright. Tapping the frame near the corner, he looked down at me again. "KH." His finger rested on the initials I'd left. "Kirstin Hill. I should have guessed."

I shrugged.

"These are really good."

"Thanks. I had fun with them."

"Did you study art in college?"

"Some, but mostly I do it for fun. It's relaxing."

He leaned closer to the frames. "Do you sell them?"

"This?" I laughed. "No. They're just silly illustrations that make me happy. No one would want to buy them."

"Well I do."

I shoved his shoulder and walked away. "Stop it. We were making dinner, remember?"

The sense of his presence followed me as I walked back to the kitchen, so I didn't turn to see if he was coming. "What first?"

He asked if I wanted to chop onions. That was a "no way." Peppers? Nope. Knives weren't a safe choice for me.

"How do you survive?"

I pointed to the microwave.

"That's just…unacceptable."

"I go out sometimes too. So that counts as a real meal, right?"

He shook his head and then proceeded to take over my kitchen. Pretty sure my house was smiling about twenty minutes later, because it smelled good in there. I inhaled, shutting my eyes. "Oh, I forgot how good that is."

"So you have smelled home-cooked goodness in your life."

I smirked at him. "Yes, smarty-pants. My mom is actually quite good in the kitchen. Went to culinary school and everything."

"And you…"

"Can't. Just can't." I inhaled again, long and deep. "But I do miss this smell."

"Also something that's just not right." He gave his simmering sauce a quick stir and then began to slice the loaf of French bread we'd bought. "Why won't you sell me some of your art?"

"Huh?"

"It'd look good in the bakery, don't you think?"

I fixed a *you're crazy* look on him. "Why are you back to that again?"

"Because I want to buy some, and you said no. I want to know why?"

"I guess I didn't think you were serious."

"I'm serious. It'd look great."

"Why is your bakery so…" Too late to filter that one, so I blurted out the rest. "…feminine?"

"Marketing, Kirstin. It's all about the marketing. Ninety percent of my customers are female."

"Oh." I took up the butter knife and started slathering the slices he set on the space near me. "And you really want one of my pieces?"

"How about three? Or five?"

I set the knife and slice of bread I'd been working on down and turned to pin a straight look on him. "What are you after?"

"What?"

"Why are you doing this?"

"I like your art."

"No, all of this. Why did you do any of this?"

His dark eyes, still happy, and yet honest, held mine. "I don't know. Just thought we should be friends."

I continued to study him, looking for angles. For the hidden agenda that must be lurking somewhere. If he had any, he hid them well.

***

Dinner was delicious, and Ian remained...Ian. Casual. Goofy. And fun. After we ate, we cleaned up the dishes—something I was actually helpful with—and then we sifted through a few of my favorite illustrations. He picked three, all of them cartoonish watercolor recreations of scenes I'd witnessed and loved in Rock Creek. The first, Paul Rustin pushing one of his nieces on a swing in the park. His cowboy hat shaded his face enough to see his grin pointed at his wife, Suzanna, who held their baby on a bench across the park. Next, two elementary kids pedaling away on their bikes down the bricked main street, both leaning over their handlebars as if in a fierce race, their grins telling the real state of the matter. And third, the barn in the middle of town, all lit up for Christmas, with smatters of people laughing and talking under the yellowish glow of the twinkling Christmas lights.

"These are really something, Kirstin." Ian fingered the barn in the final scene—clearly his favorite.

Mine too, and I smiled at the memory of that night. There was a little bit of magic hovering over Rock Creek, and that evening, the fairy dust seemed to be extra thick. That was the night I realized that truly, I wanted this sweet little town to be home. I didn't want to blend. I wanted to fit in.

"What if I put a tag on the frames?" Ian turned to me, his hand warming my shoulder. "I'll bet people would buy these. Especially if they know they're in them—like Paul and Suzanna. Would you let me?"

I eyed him with suspicion.

"Of course, if they sold, all the money would go to you."

"No gallery fee?"

"No! That's not what I meant."

Color actually speckled his cheeks, and I was surprised to see it.

"Huh."

"You don't believe me?"

"No, that wasn't what the *huh* was for. You blushed. I didn't think you knew how."

The pink deepened into red. "Trust me. I blush."

My eyebrows shot up, and I held a *gimme* look on him.

"Nope. Not telling."

"That's not fair. I've already humiliated myself like a dozen times in front of you."

"When? I didn't see anything humiliating from you."

The man faked sincerity like a Broadway pro.

Rolling my eyes, I pushed him out the front door and followed him into the frosty night. Once in my car, he fiddled with the radio until he found something with an upbeat tempo, and started wiggling his shoulders.

"Are you…dancing?" I asked.

He held my head in a forward-facing position. "You're driving. You need to focus on that."

"But…"

"Focus, young one. Don't mind the nut in the passenger seat."

I didn't mind the nut in the passenger seat—kind of liked him there. He continued the shoulder wiggling, and

I giggled. Before I was ready—or out of chuckles—we were back at the bakery.

After a little more than an hour, we had the fire mess cleaned up. The kitchen smelled like lemons, and the oven could no longer testify to my ineptness. All was as it should be—which meant I really hadn't destroyed anything more important than a pan of Monster Cookies and a hand towel after all.

I shrugged back into my coat, and Ian walked me to my car, which I'd parked behind the alley near the back entrance to the kitchen.

"Thanks for your help," he said—zero mocking in his voice.

"Well, since I started the fire—" I let the rest go unsaid.

"Accident." He snagged my elbow and wiggled it. Then after a pause, his cheeks lifted into that little-boy grin. "So, tomorrow?"

"You're either truly brave or seriously insane."

Stuffing his hands into his jeans' pockets, he shrugged.

"You didn't give me a real answer before," I said. "Why are you doing this?"

He tipped his head. "I've seen you around. You like Rock Creek—I have proof in my newly acquired art— but sometimes you have a look…"

I waited. Nothing. "A look?"

"Yeah. Like you're standing on the outside of a shop, peeking in."

I studied him in the crisp moonlight, the puffs of our breaths friendly white clouds that mingled between us. "Are you making fun of me?"

"No, I'm totally serious. I just thought…I mean I'm pretty new around here too, and I know how different it can be to move to a small town—and I thought you could use another friend."

"A friend?"

He nodded, his cheeky grin faltering for just a moment, as if he was suddenly unsure of himself.

I sighed, leaning against the hood of my car. "Yeah. I could use a friend."

The white moonglow gave enough light for me to see his face pull into a frown—an honest frown that looked very much out of place on this face I'd begun to memorize.

"I didn't mean to—" He cleared his throat, rubbed the back of his neck. "I mean, that wasn't supposed to be…condescending."

My teeth nipped at my bottom lip. "Like I'm pathetic?"

"I didn't mean that."

"Sure."

One half a step brought him closer. "Honest. I didn't. I'm sorry…I'm just…"

I waited, wondering if a rose color was heating his cheeks in the chilly night air.

"I'm just a big goofball. I told you that, right?"

"I heard that somewhere, yeah."

"Okay, good. So I can play the *goofball moment* card, and we can move on?"

Standing up, I slipped around to the driver's-side door. "Sure. Only if I get an unending allotment of *kitchen-fail* cards in return."

His hand moved in the space between us and hovered. "Deal."

We shook on it.

"Friends, then?" he asked.

I slid my palm from his and curled my fingers into a fist. A bump of our knuckles sealed the deal.

The kitchen-fail girl and the big goofball guy were friends. Rock Creek was definitely settling into home.

***

"Break time." Anastacia floated into my classroom, arm outstretched as she passed through the door, reaching for me. "I want details."

Snatching my arm, she pulled me to the big round table I kept at the back of my classroom for small group huddles. She plunked down onto one of my mini student chairs and motioned for me to do the same.

"These chairs are tiny. We could go to the teachers' lounge."

"You're not likely to talk in there. I just saw Mr. Meyers slip in with his lunch bag."

She had a point. I wasn't talking about Ian with Nolan Meyers lurking around, overhearing my humiliating tale of flames and smoke, misconstruing the whole situation. As it was, Anastacia Campbell was clearly misconstruing the situation, and I hadn't even said anything yet.

"Ready, go." Her perky wave was meant to urge me along.

"First, let's understand what this is and what it isn't. Mostly what it isn't."

"Oh?" The lift of her brows challenged my claim before I even made it.

"It isn't anything gooey."

"It's a bakery…"

"You know what I meant."

"And Ian Connealy is the baker."

"Anastacia, quit grinning like that. It looks silly."

"And he asked you to let him teach you how to bake."

"You're right." I leaned back in my tiny chair. "It's a good thing this conversation isn't happening in the teachers' lounge. Do you know how many ways what you just said could be twisted?"

"Pshh." She waved me off and sat back, twisting open the cap on her metal water bottle as she settled in for a story. "It's just us, and I don't really think that kind of thing about either of you. But you have to admit, it is a little bit...romantic of him."

"See, this is why we needed to clarify your misguided ideas. I set his kitchen on fire."

Those perfectly formed eyebrows arched, and she grinned. "Well then…"

I shook my head and gripped her wrist. "I'm not kidding here. I *literally* set the oven on fire. There was zero romance involved."

"You mean, like actual flames?"

"And smoke. And a charred towel to evidence my sad kitchen skills."

She leaned in. "Oh my gosh! What did you do?"

"Doused the flames with the fire extinguisher—which makes a big mess, by the way—while he stood there with his mouth hanging open."

Sitting there, her mouth hanging open, Anastacia blinked. "What happened next?"

"He insisted we make dinner at my house, because his kitchen wasn't usable, and he didn't think I should eat microwaved food on a regular basis."

Blue eyes widened. "You went back to your house and made dinner?"

"Tame those wild ideas, lady. It wasn't like that. He's a…"

Her lips slapped shut. "Oh. You don't like him."

"I didn't say that. I was going to say he's a goofball. A hilarious goofball, and we had fun. But not the romantic kind of fun—and that's just fine. Don't ruin it."

"Don't ruin it?" The question came out slow, her eyebrows dipping in. "How would I ruin it?"

"By trying to make it into something that it just isn't. I like him. He's fun."

"But there's nothing else there?"

I held a hand up. The simplicity of Ian's offer of friendship, with a large side helping of comedic experience, was safe. As I'd driven home from the bakery the night before, I'd latched on to it. I liked uncomplicated. Easy. It left room for me to just be me, without any pretenses involved. Muddying the easiness of it with unrealistic hopes and silly expectations seemed…dumb.

"Okay, Kirstin." Her grin mellowed into sincerity, rather than flighty dreams. "I won't ruin it. But I do want to hear about this goofballness. And also, how you set the kitchen on fire."

That I could do.

Chapter 9

"Suzanna Rustin bought that painting."

I stopped, my hand hovering over the mixing bowl where I was measuring flour into the creamed butter and eggs. "What?"

"That illustration you did of Paul and Kiera? She recognized what it was right away and asked if she could buy it. I hadn't even put tags on them yet. She loved it."

Ian's face gleamed pride, and as he moved near me to check on my progress—he'd kept a much closer eye on me over the week as we worked together after school—he bumped my shoulder with his elbow. "What'd I tell you?"

"She actually paid money for it?"

"Gladly." His nod was aimed at the mixing bowl, and then he stepped around the island. "I'm checking out front. You've got this, right?"

"Uh…" I was dumb-whipped. Seriously. Never in my wildest daydreams had I thought someone would actually want to *buy* one of my paintings. They were just me…being me. Caricatures—not even really realistic. They were fun, cutesy imitations of the things in life that made me smile. But that was all.

Until Ian…

My teeth sank into my bottom lip as my smile grew. Who knew? I continued to work, adding cinnamon and other spices to the snickerdoodle dough and mixing slowly, just like Ian had shown me. When the dough was sticky—not too dry, but not too wet—I began dipping out measured, evenly spaced balls onto the papered tray. The sheet was large, so twenty-four cookies fit neatly on one spread. I finished preparing them and slid them into the oven, setting the timer on my phone before I slipped out of the kitchen to help Ian in the front.

He was ringing up a couple I recognized from church, so I grabbed the rag from behind the register and moved to wipe down the tables. After the second table, I paused, stood straight, and studied the exposed brick wall where Ian had hung my work.

Only two. Because Suzanna Rustin *paid money* to have the third. The thrill buzzed inside my brain and tickled through my arms. I couldn't wait to call my mom.

"Hi, Miss Hill!" A little voice followed the tinkling bell that announced her entry. I turned to find little Sydney White.

"Well, hello there, Syd." I smiled—I'd already been smiling. Grinning like an Olympic champion. "How are you?"

"I'm awesome. I didn't know you worked here."

"Well, I…"

"Miss Hill helps me out after school." Ian leaned on the counter, speaking toward Sydney. "Isn't that great?"

Sydney nodded, her ponytail bouncing with both her head movement and her skipping to the pastry case. "Yeppers. Who wouldn't want to work with all these cupcakes? Smart lady, Miss Hill."

Joe and Kale, both trailing behind her, snickered.

"I hear you are the fastest girl in the first grade," I said, walking over to the counter by the cash register and stopping next to Ian. I leaned my elbows against the surface between us, my tilt bringing me closer to Syd.

"I am!" Her delighted face suddenly scrunched. "Who told you that?"

"Mrs. Campbell. She says you're like lightning."

Sydney's glowing smile lit up again. "Thanks to no more leg braces! Hey, Mrs. Campbell is pretty, huh?"

"She's beautiful." I nodded, still tipped toward her.

"She's going to have a baby—just like my Momster."

"I heard about that."

A beep-beep-beep interrupted our conversation, and I pushed off the counter. "That means my cookies are done. I'd better rescue them so I don't burn anything this time."

Sydney's expression molded into shock. "You burned some before?"

Sighing, I shook my head. "Syd, you don't want to know."

Ian chuckled, shook my shoulders, and then spoke above my head. "Everyone burns something now and then. Hazard of the trade. I've got it, Kirstin, if you want to get the Whites their order?"

I shrugged. "Sure. What'll it be, kid?"

Sydney's mouth twisted as her nose wrinkled, her deep-thought expression. "I'm thinking..."

We waited.

She tapped her chin. "I'm thinking..."

"Okay." Kale stepped forward, gently moving her seven-year-old to the side. "While she's *thinking*, I want a Sugar Snowflake."

Nodding, I opened the pastry case. "And you, Joe?"

"Buttercream Dream."

The two cupcakes landed on the tray I had pulled out for them. Ian pushed back through the door from the kitchen, one hand supporting a plate full of fresh-out-of-the oven cookies. I inhaled.

Baked sugar…but it wasn't quite…

"I want one of those." Sydney pointed to the warm cookies.

I looked at Ian, hoping he could read the instant message I was trying to send with my mind. *Did you taste them before you brought them out?*

"I was just thinking the same thing, Syd." Ian set the plate on the counter, clearly not receiving my message. "Kirstin made them herself. This one's on the house." He set a cookie on a napkin and handed it down to her.

Sydney smiled, the gap in her front teeth adorable. "Awesome! Here we go…" She shut her eyes—drama clearly a part of her normal personality—and sank her teeth in. Paused. And then her eyes flew wide open.

The shock on her face was not the good kind.

"Oh no. Is it bad?"

She looked up at her mom, clearly not sure what to do.

"If it's bad, just spit it out, Syd. It's okay." I then turned to Ian. "Did you taste them first?"

"I watched you make them, so I didn't think there was a need."

We both snatched a cookie and bit in. Instead of cinnamon bliss, my tongue encountered the savory heat of… I didn't know what. I looked up to Ian as he wiped his mouth with a napkin.

"Chili powder."

"What?" I asked.

"You used chili powder, not cinnamon." Laughter flavored his voice.

All that fun, tingling feeling of success that had tickled through me because of the painting surprise drained. I dropped my head. "You've got to be kidding me."

"Nope."

"I'm fired."

"That'd be harsh, since I don't actually pay you."

Helpless misery surely scrawled across my face. "Why do you have chili powder in here anyway?"

"Game days," Joe said, he and Kale both chuckling. "Ian serves cinnamon rolls and chili on game days. It's become a local favorite."

Also, it was Ian's only kitchen. I'd known that. Hadn't been paying attention though. "I'm sorry, Syd. That was really gross." I took the plate and dumped the rest of the cookies into the trash.

Sydney grabbed my hand and then moved to hug me. "Mistakes happen. That's what Momster says."

Ian gave her a free Cookie Dough Blast, and they left. I went and hid in the kitchen, throwing out the full batch of nasty cookie dough and feeling defeat on my shoulders like a full bag of textbooks. I really wanted to just leave.

The Sweet Tooth closed at six, like normal, and I'd learned over the past week that Ian really could use the help during the pre-closing rush. I pasted on a smile, trying to help without causing another disaster. Twice we met in the kitchen, fetching a new tray of one flavor or another of cupcakes, and the second time, he stopped me halfway to the door. His hand cupped my chin, tipping my eyes up to meet his.

"It's not that big of a deal."

I didn't answer, because if I tried I was afraid I would cry, and that would be even more stupid. So I just brushed up my smile.

"I mean it, Kirstin. Let it go."

When the bakery was empty except for us, and all the tables, counters, and equipment were clean, I shrugged into my coat and moved toward the door.

"Hey," Ian called, leaning against the island with his backside, arms crossed. "Have you had any real food since the spaghetti?"

I shrugged. "I eat."

In a silent, more serious moment that seemed unusual for him, he studied me and then formed a pout. "You want to stay for dinner? I'm thinking lemon-pepper chicken, rice, and steamed broccoli."

It probably should have sounded delicious—any other day it would have. But my stomach hurt. "Thanks. I think I'm just going to go home and find my dignity though."

"Kirstin..." He stood straight and took a step toward me. "Just forget about it." He pulled off a nearly flawless Donnie Brasco imitation.

"Says the guy who didn't almost make a kid vomit." A wisp of a smile teased the corners of my mouth. I shook it away. "Listen—I don't think this is working."

"What's not working?"

I flung a hand toward the kitchen. "This."

"The friendship?"

I rolled my eyes, knowing he knew exactly what I was talking about. "The cupcake deal. Can't we renegotiate?"

"What are the new terms?"

"You bake them, because you're good at it, and I pay you for them, like a normal customer."

He shut one eye, as if he was calculating.

"Ian."

"Thinking. Don't interrupt."

"Ian!"

Head tipped to one side, his mouth twisted, as if he was still debating. "I'll let you know tomorrow."

"Tomorrow?"

"Yeah."

"I don't think that's a good idea. I'm trying to break up with your kitchen here. Work with me."

"My kitchen doesn't want to break up."

Rolling my eyes, I shook my head. "You're impossible."

"Goofball card."

"Good night, Ian."

"That's it?"

I waved, turning my back. Though still kind of miserable about my latest kitchen-fail, a laugh snuck through my chest and out of my mouth, the puff of white into the February night air seeming happy in spite of it all.

Ian wasn't like anyone I'd met. I kind of thought he liked it that way.

***

A set of knuckles wrapped on my classroom door two minutes after I'd sent the kids to lunch.

"Anyone home?" Ian's voice caught me off guard, and I jerked my attention up from the lesson plans I was sketching out for the following week.

Staring at him, I felt my eyes widen. "What are you doing here?"

He lifted a brown bag with Sweet Tooth stamped on the front. "Lunch. Because you need real food at least once a week."

I set my pen down and pushed away from my desk. "Don't you have a business to run?"

"I put a sign up. Says I'll be back at one."

"But it's lunchtime."

"Exactly."

"Isn't that a fairly busy time for a restaurant?"

"Usually. Unless it's closed."

Crossing my arms, I forced a scowl over the threatening expression of total joy—because what was this guy thinking? "What's in the bag?"

"Chicken salad sandwich on a toasted bagel." He handed one bag to me, keeping the other that had been hiding behind its twin.

I'd never been to the Sweet Tooth for lunch. Ian specialized in sandwiches, but only served them from 11:30 to 1:00 during weekdays, so I missed out.

The smile I'd been working to smother won over my fake frown. "What are you up to?"

"Seeing my friend, because she left a little upset last night—and I didn't even get the chance to give her a Dark and Dangerous." His eyebrows lifted. "Think she was in that kind of mood."

I opened the bag. On one side, wrapped in paper, was the sandwich he promised. On the other, a cupcake box.

Ian pulled out a chair at the little round table in the back and folded his long legs until he sat. His knees looked ridiculous, nearly touching his chest. I chuckled at the picture, filing it in my mind so that I could paint it later, and slipped into a chair across from him. He opened his lunch sack and pulled out his sandwich, leaving me to do the same. I did, but paused before I took my first bite.

"This was nice of you. Thanks."

He winked, wiped his mouth with a napkin he'd pulled from the lunch sack, and then cleared his throat.

"About that renegotiation…"

"Ah, we're at the ploy." I licked a bit of chicken salad that had leaked onto my thumb. "All right, go ahead. I'm listening."

"I think maybe you're right. This isn't working."

Unexpectedly, a sagging downward spiral of disappointment sank through me. I glossed it over with a smile. "I'm glad you're reasonable, even if you are a goofball."

"Not so much reasonable…just don't want to be—"

I waited. He didn't finish. "Be?"

"I don't want you to feel miserable. That wasn't what I was going for, and if you hate baking, there's nothing wrong with that."

It wasn't that I hated it. Well, actually, yeah, I usually hated it. Except, I didn't hate hanging out in Ian's kitchen. Thus the sad falling sensation of more disappointment.

"Actually, lunch is kind of an apology." Ian shifted in the little chair, moving his legs so that they poked out straight, which looked much more comfortable. "I didn't mean to make you think that you should be different— that you should be anything other than you. I'm sorry if that's how I made you feel."

Was that how I felt? Sometimes, yeah. Especially now that I so badly wanted to be a real part of this town. But I didn't really feel like I should be different because of Ian. With him, I pretty much felt like…me. And I liked it.

"You didn't, but thanks."

"You know you're pretty amazing at other things, right? Like those paintings. And from what I hear from Keegan and from other people, you're a great teacher."

Who couldn't smile at that? "Thanks."

"So do what you do. You know? I'll take care of the cupcakes, so don't worry about it."

"I'll pay you."

"Nah. Pretty sure I owe you for all your free help at the bakery."

"Help? Are you using that word loosely there?"

His hallmark full-toothed smile spread wide. "Maybe just a little—although you were helpful in the front. So thanks for that."

I sat back, took a bite of chicken salad on a bagel, which was amazing, by the way, and thought. The week had been fun. Even with the fire. And the chili powder thing. And humiliation on the side. Hanging out with Ian was fun. I hated to see that stop.

"So that brings us to the renegotiation part."

My gaze had drifted toward the floor, although I didn't realize it, because I wasn't really seeing anything other than Ian's antics, which had made their own caricatures in my mind. Him slipping the hair net over my face the first day. His face after I'd doused the fire. Him juggling in the store…

"Hello? Kirstin Hill, are you present?"

I shook a little and then sat up. "Here."

"Good. Let's talk terms."

"About what?"

"This friendship. And my kitchen. It still doesn't want a breakup, and I vote no on that too. You actually laugh at my weirdness, so I think you should stick around."

I had no words. Just an amused smirk.

"Deal?"

"What do I get out this?"

"Hours of unending entertainment."

True. And definitely worth it. This wasn't even actually a negotiation anyway, and I was pretty sure he knew he'd had me at *I think you should stick around.*

"I'll throw in an endless supply of free cupcakes. Just don't spread that around. Gotta make a living."

"I think I'll need new pants."

His *I won* expression had that eight-year-old-boy quality to it. "I'm going to take that as a yes."

"You might regret it."

Smashing his lunch sack into a packed ball, he shook his head and then launched it toward the trash can by the door, free-throw style. "I seem to recall hearing that before."

"Yes. Shortly before I set the oven on fire."

"Don't regret that."

"Your bakery could have gone up in flames."

He shrugged. "I checked my insurance policy. There's no kitchen-fail-women-who-start accidental-fires exclusion on it, so we're good." The laughter in his eyes shone as he kept his gaze on me.

Suddenly I remembered how handsome Ian, the goofball baker, was. And also that he was sitting there staring at me. Smiling.

I might have drooled a little.

Chapter 10

So I helped him. Every day after school for the following week, I worked the front counter—with him often at my side, because, reality check—Ian's cupcakes weren't the only draw into the Sweet Tooth.

Marketing. He was pretty good at it.

Realizing that little piece of nonfiction wove a strange sensation of…something not exactly pleasant, but strong. Maybe I should have spent more time considering whatever that strong reaction twisting silently inside of me was, but mostly I was too busy grinning at the man who made everyone smile.

And also, in my diminishing spare time, when I wasn't doing lesson plans, grading papers, working extra duties at school, helping out at the bakery, or eating food that didn't come from a microwave with Ian, I was painting.

Something inside me came alive. Whenever I was alone at home, the little table I'd set up in my spare bedroom tugged at me, the canvass and paints whispering *Come play, Kirstin…* It'd become an irresistible, beautiful addiction. Maybe addiction wasn't the right word, but I seemed to take flight with a brush in my hand, a scene in my mind, and a blank page waiting eagerly to be filled.

I liked color. Bright, happy color. The scenes were lighthearted and endearing, making me smile.

I was smiling a lot. It was like the best version of me began to sprout and grow. Or perhaps it was the true version of me. The things that had nagged at me before, especially after I'd first moved to Rock Creek, faded. I didn't spend nearly as much time wondering if I'd ever fit into this cute little town that had slipped into my heart. And the sad feeling of failure—of being so weird that I couldn't do kitcheny things like every other normal woman I knew? Hardly felt it at all. Even when I was hanging out in the kitchen with Ian.

Those little nips of insecurities—they just…

I didn't know. Something had changed.

My days at school, I found it easier to interact with my fellow teachers and the paras I worked with. I stopped thinking of myself as the new girl, the outsider. I was just Kirstin. Miss Hill. At the Sweet Tooth, interacting with Ian's customers was like talking to my neighbors—and sometimes they actually were. Easy and normal.

One night, as I painted a scene of the bakery—one where Ian had said something hilarious, and the customers all grinned or laughed—I painted myself into the scene. Standing beside the cash register, across from Joe, Kale, and Sydney White, smiling.

I fit in. Just as…me.

I called that painting *Homecoming*. Ian picked it out as one of the two paintings he wanted to hang up next, to replace the two that had sold.

"Okay," I said. "But you can't sell that one."

He looked back at it, his eyes a little bit lit, and he traced the image behind the glass of the frame, his fingers brushing over the caricature of me. Something in his smile pulled at my chest—sparking this weird sensation of ache and joy.

When he looked down at me, he nodded. And that was all.

***

The first Sunday in February dawned in a glitter of frost and dressed in white. Though the snow had held off during the previous week, the frigid temperatures had remained. The low-hanging clouds puffed with the promise of more snow, but that morning I smiled at the thought as I walked to church.

I looked forward to slipping into my place at the back, grinning a hello at Sydney White and her parents a few rows up. Finding Anastacia and Mitch Campbell and hearing about how the nursery painting was going, and trying to suppress a secret grin of my own as I thought about the set of caricatures I was working on as a gift for their baby's room.

Also, I looked forward to seeing Ian. My friend.

Before I slid into the seat in the back that I'd claimed as my own shortly after I'd moved to Rock Creek, he found me in the front gathering area before the music started, just as he had for the past couple of weeks. According to the pattern newly established, we'd chat for a few minutes about my lesson plans, and paintings, and the latest flavor of cupcake he was thinking he might add to his menu, as well as several other nonrelated and unimportant topics.

Like his obsession with the old *Peanuts* cartoons and his carefully selected collection of authentic vintage *Peanuts* strips. He didn't collect much in the way of paraphernalia—because he didn't want to have to dust them. Although, he did have three metal lunch boxes featuring Snoopy and the gang. Mostly he sought out the original newsprint strips—something his grandfather had collected and passed on.

Ian was an endless adventure into the quirky.

That Sunday, however, we didn't have the opportunity to dip into the peculiarities of our likes and dislikes. (He thought it was bizarre that I hated brussel sprouts. Now you truly know the depth of his weirdness.) Trailing behind Ian when he sought me out was an adorable woman whose light-red hair made her peacock-blue eyes seem almost unreal. Hand to her back, the man behind this little forest fairy made me snap a double take.

It was Ian. Only Ian was Ian. I was seeing double Ians.

The real Ian smiled knowingly. "Don't freak out. There's really only one me. My brother just stole my face because he's completely unoriginal."

The other Ian—whose smile didn't say goofball as much as it said calm, rational, and maybe just a tad bit dry—shook his head. "I'm the older one, so don't listen to him."

Ian plopped an arm around my shoulders and squeezed. "Kirstin, meet my brother, Connor."

Blinking, I looked from Ian to Connor and back again.

"I'm better looking, right?" Ian said.

I raised my eyebrows.

"That's okay. You can tell me later. After you've had a chance to study us."

Heat brushed over my face.

The red-haired forest fairy chuckled. "Good to see you haven't changed, Ian." She reached across the space to shake my hand. "I'm Morgan. Connor's wife." She winked as I slid my hand into hers. "And just so you know, I married the better-looking brother. But you don't have to say it."

My wit couldn't keep up with them, and I couldn't help staring at Connor. It was dumb—I'd seen twins before—but to see Ian's face on another guy, and yet it wasn't Ian, was frankly bizarre.

"You didn't say twin." I looked up at Ian. "You said you had a brother."

Morgan snickered. "Trust me—that little omission of his has landed Ian in trouble more than once."

Ian's cheeks streaked with a little bit of red.

Interesting.

He recovered, narrowed a look on me, and changed the subject. "How about you come over for dinner after service?"

"Do I get to hear about this alleged trouble?"

His eyebrows did a weird slanting thing, and he rubbed his neck. "You might have to be sworn in first."

"What on earth?"

Leaning closer, Ian whispered, "You know how you don't want the whole town to know that you set my kitchen on fire?"

Heat touched my face now too, and I eyed him.

"I don't want everyone to know what a dating disaster I am. So as long as you swear, under oath, that you'll never tell…"

That got my attention. "Dating disaster?"

"Not here," he hissed, one of his big hands suddenly covering my mouth. "It's not safe."

Morgan rolled her eyes and snorted. "Ian. You're such a goober."

He grinned. Like he'd won first prize in a contest. Maybe he had.

Chapter 11

After church service I made my way to the bakery, parking in the alley. I slipped through the kitchen door in the back, closing it because the snow was coming down harder. When I turned around, the two brothers were both leaning against the island counter, both with their legs crossed and arms folded. I studied them. Same build, same dark hair, same dark eyes, same facial features. They were truly identical. And yet I knew exactly which one was Ian. The expression on his face was unmistakable. While Connor was pleasant, his mouth somewhat upturned, his countenance was more serious. It was a look I'd seen on Ian only a couple of times—the first, when he'd lifted my chin and told me not to worry about the chili powder cookies. The second, in my classroom, when he'd worried that he made me feel like I needed to be different and apologized for it.

Yes, Connor and Ian were identical in looks, but though they'd both changed from their button-down dress shirts they'd worn to church, I knew exactly who was who, and I locked eyes with Ian, grinning.

"Impressive," Morgan said as she came through the door from the storefront. "Only a handful of people can pick out who is who on a glance."

Ian stood up from the counter and stepped toward me. "It was my more muscular build that tipped you off, wasn't it?"

Connor snorted. "Dream on. More like that baker's-man belly you've been packing on."

Ian patted his stomach, pushing out his belly in a ridiculous attempt to grow a nonexistent cupcake gut. Turning to one side so that I could see his profile, he set a false devastated plea on me. "Say it ain't so, Kirstin. Say it ain't so."

The man was adorably silly. I shook my head. "No, and that's not funny, because I actually do need new jeans, thanks to your cupcakes."

Connor stepped forward, gripping his brother's shoulders and leaning around him. "It was my irresistible look of pure intelligence, wasn't it?"

Morgan came next to her husband, arm slipping around his waist. "He's so humble, isn't he?"

"Shockingly." I laughed. Shrugging off my coat, I moved toward Ian's office to hang it up. "Not quite, Connor. But it was your expressions. Ian always looks like he's got a comic strip reeling through his mind."

Ian met me before I went into his office, taking my coat for me.

"Probably he does," Morgan said, her voice smiling. "Has he shown you his comic strip collection?"

"Not yet," I answered, "but I've heard about it."

Ian squeezed my shoulder as he slipped from his office behind me and then moved toward the oven on the opposite side of the kitchen, rolling his sleeves to his forearms as he walked. "I just need to cook the noodles and mix the sauce, and we'll be ready."

Morgan inhaled. "Ah. Ian's fettuccini." She glanced at her husband. "Maybe we should move here. I'm remembering how good your brother's food is."

Connor grinned. "You might have a point."

I wondered if they were serious about a move, but as I stood there watching Ian work, I felt a nudge of guilt because he was fixing dinner for all of us while we did nothing. But the whole kitchen-fail thing...another dilemma. How much did I want to humiliate myself in front of Ian's family?

"So, Kirstin." Connor interrupted my internal debate. "Ian says you help him out here after school."

Fantastic. Ian already told. Well, guess that made my decision a lot easier. I walked into the middle of the U made by the counters and ovens. "*Help* is a pretty loose term," I said to Connor and then tapped Ian's arm with the back of my hand. "But if you give me something that doesn't involve too much mixing or any fire, I'd love to help you with lunch."

Ian looked down at me and winked. "I have some lettuce, tomatoes, and cucumbers already washed and chopped in the ice box. You want to mix them for a salad?"

"Ah, you prepared for me." I patted his back. "Very wise."

"What's this?" Morgan moved toward the walk-in refrigerator with me, obviously willing to help as well.

Oh. So he hadn't told.

"I'm not trustworthy in the kitchen."

Ian snorted.

"Fine." I faked a dramatic sigh. "I'm a disaster. A total kitchen-fail. I don't know why Ian lets me in here."

Morgan grinned, a sly, *I think I know why* kind of grin, which pulsed a sense of awkward through me. If it'd been Anastacia, I would have poked her shoulder and mouthed *don't ruin it* to her while Ian's back was still turned to us. But Morgan was a near stranger—and clearly had made some assumptions.

"Can't be that bad," Connor said from across the kitchen. He had taken a loaf of Italian bread that had been wrapped and waiting on the counter and was running a knife through it, making thick slices.

I waited for Ian to respond. When he didn't, I was forced to confess while Morgan and I unpacked salad fixings and dumped them into a glass bowl I'd pulled from one of the cabinets.

"I set Ian's oven on fire with a towel."

Both Morgan and Connor laughed.

"It was an accident," Ian said.

"I baked snickerdoodles with chili powder instead of cinnamon."

"Another accident."

Connor and Morgan continued to chuckle. I turned so that I faced the center of the kitchen with them, and Ian stood at an angle to the stove so that he could whisk the sauce while we talked. Smart. I would have walked away and burned the stuff.

This was why I didn't cook.

I caught the suspicious glances both Connor and Morgan had cast between Ian and me. Thought I should just clear this whole deal up. "It's so bad that I've even scared off men with my kitchen accidents." I air quoted the word *accidents.*

Morgan's eyebrows darted upward. "What?"

Ian looked at me, mostly amusement in his eyes, but also something else. His glance didn't stay on me long enough for me to figure it out, but I chalked it up to curiosity.

"Not kidding. My sister thought that she should introduce me to one of her husband's friends from work, so they had us both over for dinner one night last summer. She made a roast, and everything was almost ready, when my ten-month-old nephew decided he was hungry. Paige asked me to whip up the gravy while she fed Caleb. I gave her my best *are you insane* look while the guys were doing whatever they were doing, but she just waved me off. 'Follow the instructions, and you'll be fine,' she said. I swear I followed those instructions…" I shook my head, feeling heat pool in my cheeks.

"What happened?" Morgan asked.

"We sat down to eat, and the gravy was awful. I'm talking make-you-want-to-vomit awful. Paige asked me what happened, and I was all, 'I don't know! I did what your directions told me to do.' Then she got this look— the *oh my goodness, no* look.

"'What'd you use for milk?' she asked.

"'Milk?' I answered.

"'Which milk?'

"I shrugged, now completely irritated as well as totally embarrassed.

"'The milk in the smaller jug?' she asked.

"'Yes…' I said.

"Paige stood up and began clearing plates, because we'd all smothered our roasts and potatoes with the puke-worthy gravy. 'That was baby formula, Kirstin.'" I face-palmed my head as I paused the story, still mortified by it.

Ian tipped his head back and let a full belly laugh roll. "That. Is. Awesome."

Morgan and Connor were laughing as well, and I couldn't help but chuckle too, even though my face had to have been tomato red.

"So yeah. He never called, and I told my sister to *never* do that again. She thought it was hilarious."

The sauce ready, Ian moved it from the stove and let it rest on a pad waiting on the counter. "He never called? What a chicken."

"I agree," Morgan said, grabbing the pot of noodles from the stove top to drain them. "That's just bad luck."

Ian nudged my shoulder. "See, I keep telling you."

I lifted an eyebrow. "I have a lot of bad luck."

Connor crossed from his spot near the island and dropped an arm around my shoulders. "Don't worry about it, kid. My brother here could probably match your kitchen-fails one for one with dating-disaster stories."

There it was again… I narrowed my look on Ian, and though his shoulders moved with a silent chuckle, his ears lit with a warm red.

"Hang on now. You didn't tell me anything about this."

He shook his head. "There's a reason."

I crossed my arms. "Not. Fair."

"Connor's right. I could easily match your stories with one dating catastrophe or another. It's pretty bad."

"Such as…" I waited, tapping my foot, although my grin certainly gave away my amusement.

Ian rubbed a hand over his head, looking at the floor. "Where to even begin?"

Morgan laughed. "How about with the twin problems? We ran into that blonde you went out with, by the way. She glared at Connor and then looked at me. Next thing I know, she's stepping in front of us, and after she shoved Connor's shoulder, she turned to me and said, 'I think you should know that your husband is a cheater. I went out with him three times. He never once mentioned having a wife.'"

"Oh no," Ian groaned. "I'm sorry."

"Wait. Back up. What happened?"

"I met this woman at a coffee shop back home, and I asked her out. We hit it off pretty well, so we went out two more times. Then a few days after our third date, I got a text from her calling me a scumbag. Said she saw me making out with my wife at the theater—*I saw the rings, jerk.*" He air quoted her snarky accusation and shook his head. "I texted her back telling her that would be my brother, Connor, and his wife, Morgan. I got a one-word reply, but I won't repeat it."

"Why didn't you tell her you had a twin brother earlier?"

Ian spread his arms, palms up. "Do you give a family lineup on the first date?"

I shook my head, still laughing.

"Exactly. Besides, I think it's Connor's fault. Aren't you two a little old to be making out in a theater?"

Morgan's cheeks glowed, but she tugged her husband's shirtfront, and he leaned down to take her mouth with his quite willingly.

"Ah, come on, man. Not in my kitchen."

"Marriage is good, brother." Connor spoke in between noisy, exaggerated kisses. "You should try it."

"That would require more than three dates. And stop. Seriously. I'm getting a little sick over here."

The smoochers broke apart, looking exceptionally pleased with themselves.

"That's just one unreasonable woman," I said, moving closer to Ian as he lifted plates from the open shelving near his head.

"Oh, she's not the only one. Have you tried Tinder?"

"No. Not brave enough. Plus, isn't that a little…uh, sketchy?"

"Yes—depends on where you come from. And keep it that way. My buddy told me to try it. 'Make sure you put down that you're a funny guy,' he said. 'Women love a guy with a good sense of humor.' Apparently, though, putting down good humor attracts the nearly crazy ones. I had one woman meet me at a coffee shop—you know, because that's a safe way to start a Tinder date—and she came in, looked me over, and got this look of relief. So I thought that was a good sign, until she slid into the bench across from me and said, 'I was so nervous because your picture made you look like a ten, and I'm a solid eight. I figured this was going to be a waste of time. But now I see that you're really an eight, so I feel much better.'"

My chin fell open. "Nah-uh. She said that?"

"Word for word, I swear. And then she told me that maybe if I worked out a little more and ditched the hat, I'd be a niner. A. Niner!"

Morgan patted his back. "She's crazy. Connor's a solid ten, so that would mean you're at least a niner."

Rolling his eyes, Ian stepped to the side and motioned to the food. "It'll get cold before I run out of stories, so we should pray and eat."

Connor nodded, and before I knew what to do next, he was praying.

"God, you're good. Thanks for the food and the friends and the family. Right now I'm thankful that you make us different. Help us to embrace that, to laugh sometimes and to build each other up in all of it. And thanks for a brother who can cook so we don't starve. Amen."

Somewhere in the middle of that easygoing, sincere prayer, I felt the little ball of tension in my middle uncoil. I couldn't imagine Ian with a run of dating disasters. He was too nice. Too much fun. And yet...

It almost made me like him more. Like his quirks were even more endearing—and it was fascinating that he was laughing right alongside his brother about it. I remembered him telling me the week before to *just do what you do*. That was pretty much how he lived, and the freedom he had to be who God made him was like a certificate of release to me.

Once again I found that I could be me, complete with failures and little quirks, and it was totally cool.

I was thankful for Ian—but not just because he could cook. Also, I wasn't sure what was wrong with those other women. He was definitely a ten.

Chapter 12

Sunday dinner had been charming. Easygoing laughter and a few more stories—like the one where Ian gave Tinder another shot, and when he met the woman, once again at a coffee shop, she looked him over and told him they needed to go shopping. He asked why, and she said that his shirt clashed with her outfit, so he needed to buy something different. After staring at her for five full seconds, waiting for her to crack a smile and say *just kidding*, he said, "How about I buy you a coffee and then I'll drop you off at the mall?"

She didn't think that was funny.

I thought the whole thing was hysterical, even if I did feel bad for Ian. He quit Tinder after the mall-woman fiasco, because who was really up for that nonsense? He'd pretty much given up on dating after that.

That announcement pressed a little bit of gloom into my heart, and I wrestled with the reason for that unexpected reaction every day the following week. It took some work to beat the sadness back while I was working with him at the bakery, and for some reason my attention would snag on that illustration I'd called *Homecoming* that Ian had hung on the exposed brick wall in the dining area. I saw him. And me. Then me. And him.

I think maybe I wanted to see *him and me*. But that thought was formless, wordless. Without real understanding or meaning. So I pushed it away for the rest of the week.

We'd worked on the cupcakes after closing. And when I say we, what I mean is Ian mixed the batter and then let me dip it into the muffin tins. He'd bake them, and once they were cool, I'd remove them from the tins and line them up on a sheet that he'd place in the freezer.

"We'll wait to frost them until Friday night," he said. "You're participating in that event, so bring your best game."

"I have no game," I responded dryly.

"I'm not frosting six hundred cupcakes alone on a Friday night."

"Six hundred? I ordered two."

"I promise you, Kirstin. Two hundred will not be enough."

I tried to wrap my mind around frosting six hundred cupcakes, as well as Ian's generosity in donating six hundred cupcakes, because he insisted I was not paying for them. Whether I understood it or not, he was doing it, and there was no way I was letting him do it alone.

Each evening would end with Ian asking me, "How about some dinner. On me."

I agreed, except on Thursday, to which he scowled. "Missing your microwave dinners?"

"No, but I'm fully addicted to this show. I can't miss it. I'll go into withdrawal, and then my angry alter ego will emerge, and I'm pretty sure we won't be friends anymore."

"That'd be tragic." He chuckled. "What would happen if I called you during said show?"

"I wouldn't answer."

"Even if I kept hitting Resend?"

"You'd be put on silent."

That ornery eight-year-old-boy expression spread over his face. "But not blocked?"

Block Ian Connealy's calls? Probably not in this life. Or the next. I smiled at him, shrugging into one sleeve of my coat, but didn't answer, because I wasn't sure how that kind of a comment would be taken. Wasn't sure how I meant it...

Ian moved to hold the other half of my coat, slipping the sleeve I hadn't pushed an arm through over my shoulder. "I won't press my luck."

I left, everything normal and light between us. He did call me that night, but just to make sure I got home okay in the snow.

But the next day, everything went so-not-normal. My most epic kitchen disaster was about to unravel.

So there we were at the bakery on the Friday night before the dance. Ian sang Elton John's "I'm Still Standing" in time with the mixer across the kitchen. Badly.

The man couldn't hold a tune with a pair of tongs. But it was still...

Adorable.

I slid a look over my shoulder at him, and he caught it with a sheepish grin. The shy one that also was a little bit like *oh, you heard that? Thanks for noticing...* He slipped a wink at me and went back to his very off version of the song, complete with a little shake of his shoulders in line with what I assumed was some kind of coherent rhythm in his head.

"Music is about as dangerous in your hands as pastry is in mine," I said.

"It's not *that* bad."

I turned to face him, feigning outrage. "Excuse me?"

"You can decipher what I'm butchering, right?" He smiled wider, letting me fill in the rest of the comparison.

"Hey, I'm getting better. Sydney was actually willing to taste one of my cookies the other day, and she said—this is a quote—'It's not too bad, Ms. Hill.' So there you go."

"Did you tell her you were under close supervision when you baked them?"

I tried, really tried, I promise, to put on a mean scowl. It must have turned out more like a facial tick, because Ian burst into a belly laugh and then started right back where he'd left off, moving to his own unpredictable beat. Next thing I knew, he had me in hand, wiggling around the kitchen in a tribal sort of dance that would probably frighten children.

"Stop." I gasped between laughs. "Just stop, before you hurt one of us."

He chuckled again, spun me out and then in, caught me near his shoulder, which frankly shocked me speechless, and then bent me backward into a dip.

I laughed so hard I couldn't right myself, and the man wasn't any help at all because he chose not to be. He simply held me half upside down with a highly amused smirk.

"So there you go," he mimicked.

I grasped at his shoulder until I found a grip—it took three tries—and scrambled my way back to a bipedal posture. "You are a nut."

Now standing straight, he went back to the frosting that he'd been whipping in the stand mixer. He shot me a sideways glance, a smile still curving his mouth.

I think that was when it happened. Pretty sure. Or maybe that was when I realized something had already happened and I'd been blindly unaware of the change. Either way, one moment I was standing there still giggling at his antics and the next…

Holy sweet cream. What the cupcakes? Oh. My. Triple-chocolate-chip cookies.

Ian continued on with his normal, everyday, nothing's-going-on-with-him life. I scurried back to the other counter, which faced the opposite way of the man who'd apparently just dipped me into a new and bizarre—though not entirely unpleasant—yet really perplexing dimension.

I'm in love with him…

Seriously. That was what I thought standing there with the blood filtering back down from my head. *I'm in love with Ian. And not just because the man feeds me.*

This was a very awkward moment. Just in case you've never experienced this, let me try to describe it.

Let's say that there's this…uh…cupcake. Yeah. We'll go with that. There's this cupcake. It's a good-looking cupcake. A very good-looking cupcake. You admire it. It's nice. The cake part looks moist. The frosting is piled on thick and creamy and arranged just exactly so. It's a lovely cupcake, and you don't mind admitting that you like to maybe just stare at that cupcake when no one is looking. But that's about it. You appreciate the cupcake, and you look at it. A lot.

But then you suddenly feel it. Your tongue seems to swell, and there's way more saliva in your mouth than necessary. All your thoughts suddenly and inexplicably zero in on that cupcake. You must HAVE that cupcake. No one else can have it, only you, and it's rather urgent because…

You think you might be in love with the baker.

No, wait. That's not how…

Oh never mind. Here's the thing. Ian and I, we were friends. Friendly kind of friends. The can-tease-each-other kind because it's light and fun and never really that deep. The kind that can carry on an easy conversation over the phone because you're bored, but then, when say…that show that you're addicted to (ahem, hello BBC drama) comes on, it's perfectly fine to say, "Hey, gotta go. My show's on." And he's like "See ya." And that's it. It's comfortable. Easy. And not…

Romantic.

Romantic is complicated and messy. I left the city because I wanted clean and simple. I was good with Ms. Hill for the rest of my life because it was exactly the opposite of complicated—and not at all laced with expectations that were most likely doomed to failure. Even my name was simple—and I liked that.

Kirstin Connealy… Huh. Not really that much more complicated.

Great puffs of flour, where had that come from?

"Pretty sure that frosting is already dead."

I started, my spine ramming straight, but I didn't dare look at the man teasing me. What if my thoughts somehow sprawled out on my forehead? What if God had suddenly hung thought bubbles over me and Ian could read them?

"What?" I stammered, not turning toward him.

"The frosting you're beating?"

His presence neared. Not good.

No, good. Very good… Somewhere in this insanity, I'd sprouted a new head voice. She sounded like Marilyn Monroe, with her come-hitherish drawl. I shook my head, trying to erase her, as if my mind were an Etch A Sketch.

"The frosting is going to taste like cardboard if you keep whipping it like that." His hand covered mine, stilling my whisk, and stayed there.

My heart suddenly decided it could keep rhythm about as well as Ian. Sporadic spurts of sprinting and dying alternated while he just held his hand there. On mine. As if it were necessary.

I swallowed and then pushed out a voice that I begged the Creator of all things would sound like my normal sass. "What are you doing?"

"Saving your cupcakes."

Oh, you can save my— Mentally, I slapped a hand over the Monroe vixen who was being sultry-obnoxious. She wasn't helping. At all.

"Back off, baker." I elbowed him lightly, thinking that was a move that I would have pulled in pre-lovestruck moments.

His free hand caught my arm and wiggled it. "Hoping for another dance?"

I could picture his teasing smile, even if I wasn't willing to look up to find it. "I knew it. Just can't resist."

Yeah, not touching that one. *You either, Marilyn.*

I took a very tiny step away from him. To be subtle. "Is the oven still on?"

"Is that a real question?"

Because duh. Yeah. The baker has his oven on. Been on all day, and we had fifty more cupcakes to bake. "I think you set it too high. It's like a volcano in here."

He leaned around my shoulder, his face popping into my line of vision. One eyebrow cocked. "Can't handle the heat?"

No. Actually I couldn't.

"It's like five hundred degrees."

The other eyebrow joined its arched companion. "Hot flashes? Aren't you a little young?"

I took another, much bigger step away from him and snatched a hand towel from the end of the counter. "I need some air. I'm gonna melt."

"Kirstin, are you—"

Okay? Nope. Clearly not. *Crazy?* Yep. Clearly so.

I wasn't sure which option he'd picked to ask, because I hustled my little hiney outta that roaster, hoping he'd stay put until I could get my cupcake cravings under control. And Marilyn boxed up and shipped back to the land of the ridiculous.

The cool February air smacked my cheeks, as if to knock some sense back into me as I stumbled my way out into the alley behind the bakery. Ripping at the knot lying on my waist, I jerked and tugged until the strings were undone and I could escape the very confining apron that seemed to be smothering me. After tugging it over my head, which did amazing things to my hair, I was sure, I wrapped both fists around it and buried my face into the fabric.

"Uggg."

Deep breaths. I just needed a few deep, calming breaths, and my old self would decide to come back. Then I could go back in there, face my friend, who probably thought I'd skipped over to the Looney Tune village, and we could laugh about it.

I pictured that.

"What was that all about?" he'd say.

I'd shrug. "Just had this insane moment where I thought I was in love with you. Don't worry. It passed."

He'd smirk and then laugh, and we'd both go back to our cupcake project.

The scene did painful things to my heart. He'd laugh at me. Straight up laugh, and that would hurt so much that I wouldn't be able to breathe.

Oh man, I was really in it. Trouble, that was.

And maybe love?

"Kirstin?" Teasing had left his voice, and now the man slipping through the back door of the bakery looked seriously concerned. "Are you okay? You're kind of making me worried."

Unravelling my balled-up apron, I fished for intelligence inside my brain. In the meantime, he continued toward me, and I was foolish enough to look into those dark eyes, all soft and gooey with concern.

What was I fishing for again?

I scowled and looked back at the wrinkled-up apron. One long, warm finger brushed under my chin and lifted my face back up to meet his gaze.

"What's going on?"

The lowness of his tone seemed…sexy. And his nearness made my pulse do that crazy, can't-hold-a-beat thing again. Without my permission, my focus slid from those melt-my-heart chocolate eyes to his lips.

Lips that smiled easily. Lips that had recently whispered my name. Lips that I wondered…

He'd been making frosting. Would they taste like frosting? There were very few things in this world as amazing as Ian's frosting.

Those lips might very well be on that short list.

"Hey." He wiggled my chin, and my gaze flew back up to his eyes. "What's going on inside that head?"

All thinking stopped. "What would you do if I kissed you?"

That was my voice. My words. Coming out of my mouth.

Oh my word… I actually asked him that! Out loud. For reals.

His hand drifted away from my chin, and Ian froze, the movement of his eyes looking frantic. Searching for a way to say that we were friends, and remember? He was done with dating. What the heck was I thinking?

My worst kitchen-fail ever, and I wasn't even in the kitchen. I gripped the fabric of the apron with both hands and raised it over my face. "That wasn't supposed to come out of my mouth, Ian. I'm sorry."

I didn't pull the apron away from my face as I turned away, hardly caring if I tripped over a pallet or something stashed in the alley. Running was the only option, and that was exactly what I did.

"Kirstin, wait."

No way. I pulled the apron from my eyes and bolted.

Chapter 13

"Help." I didn't even wait for Anastacia to finish her predictably perky *Hey, Kirstin, I'm glad to hear your voice...*

"W-what?" she stammered.

"Just say it's gonna be okay."

"Uh..."

I leaned against my steering wheel, my car parked safely in my driveway, away from the scene of my worst fail. "I'm counting on your insatiable optimism here. Just say it."

"Okay. Everything's going to be fine. Just... You'll see."

"My life is on fire here," I countered, frustration in my voice. "It's not going to be fine."

She paused for what seemed like forever, and I wondered if she was mad at me for my unfair outburst.

"Should I come over?"

"I don't know." I moaned. And then I growled, sat up, and smacked my steering wheel. "I ruined it! I told *you* not to ruin it, and then *I* went and ruined it!"

"Uh...are we talking about the cute baker?"

"He has a name."

"I know. Just gauging the situation. You sound bad. I'm on my way. Maybe I should stop at the Sweet Tooth and grab a Dark and Dangerous?"

"Not funny, Anastacia."

She let a tiny ripple of a laughter loose over the phone. "It's gonna be okay, Kirstin. I'm on my way."

The dead air in my ear told me she'd hung up, which meant that she was truly hightailing her way to my house. I should go in. Turn on the lights. Turn up the thermostat. Try to look less like the idiot who just sabotaged her best friendship ever and more like a grown-up girl. But I sat there, staring out of my windshield, still seeing the panic in Ian's eyes as he studied me.

How could I have done something so stupid? Just when I'd started feeling like Rock Creek was truly becoming home, I went and messed up the reason I was finally feeling comfortable here. Ian had shown me how to fit in, how to just...be me.

Now what? How was I supposed to just be me without him?

I rationalized through that. It seemed like a dumb question. I was the authentic me because, well, because that was who I was. Yeah, Ian drew that out—showed me the freedom of it, but did that have to change?

My heart rate settled as I exhaled slowly. The world beyond my windshield began to come back into focus. Rock Creek was a charming town, and it could be home no matter what happened between the baker and me. I didn't have to change, even if things shifted between us. Don't get me wrong. I was still pretty devastated that I wrecked such a good friendship and sore that Ian didn't seem to reciprocate what had changed in my feelings about that friendship, but there was an anchor that took hold in the middle of all of it.

I didn't have to change.

A tap at my window startled me from that little glimmer of revelation. Sucking in a breath, I glanced to my left. Anastacia stood next to my car, and as soon as we made eye contact, she made a sad face, complete with a pouty bottom lip. She stepped back, and I exited the vehicle, snagging my messenger school bag as I went.

"Bad day, huh?" She slipped her arm through mine, and we walked toward my front door.

"Just the last fifteen minutes." I unlocked the door, and she followed me in. Dumping my bag and my coat onto a bench by the entry, I turned to her and exhaled. "I asked Ian what he would do if I kissed him."

Her blue eyes took on a Frisbee quality, and then she started to grin.

"Don't. It's not cute or funny. He looked at me like I was crazy."

"What?"

"Like he didn't know what to do with me."

She grabbed my arm. "You're kidding."

"Like I ruined everything."

"But he's been flirting with you for weeks now."

I froze, settling my wild gaze on her and narrowing it. "He has not."

She laughed. One disbelieving chuckle. "Yes, Kirstin. He has."

My mind twirled with that for several breaths. It was so tempting to latch on to it. But the look on his face...

I shook my head. "Maybe that's what it looked like, but he wasn't flirting. He's given up on dating, so that wasn't it. We were good friends, and I should have been content with that."

"Kirstin…"

"No, you didn't see the look on his face when I blurted the question out. He was panicked. Didn't know what to say."

Her mouth twisted to one side, and a rare scowl wrinkled her forehead. "That just doesn't make sense."

My shoulders folded in, and I sighed.

Compassion wrote over her frown, and she stepped beside me, wrapping an arm around my shoulder. "It's gonna be okay," she whispered.

Somehow, I knew she was right, in the long run. At the moment though, I was miserable. And honestly, I kind of wanted to stay miserable.

***

Anastacia stayed until nine. When she left, I curled up on my couch and scrolled through the listings on the TV. I stalled on the Food Network and clicked Select. I never watched that station—had quite enough of it between my mom and sister while I was growing up, but seeing the kitchen on the screen seemed oddly soothing. In a heartache kind of way—like the way that song "I'll Be Home for Christmas" seemed to be. Hopeful, even if for many it was unrealistic—and yet the lovely thought was somehow comforting.

I fetched the giant giraffe my sister had given me when I'd moved to Rock Creek, and I snuggled with him while the TV flashed kitchen scenes. Talk about quirky. My sister was. Paige had a subtly different way of thinking. Like giving a giant stuffed animal to her adult younger sister as a housewarming gift. Not nearly as annoying-funny as my mother's fire extinguisher, but equally unusual.

"They remind me of you," she'd said.

I didn't get it. I was neither tall nor spotted, nor did I have a long neck. But that night as I clutched the pole neck of Jeremy the Giraffe, understanding crept into my mind.

Giraffes were unique. Really no other creature on the earth like them.

I smiled, a warm ache snagging in my chest.

My phone buzzed somewhere around ten, and I hoped it was Paige. I hadn't expected it to be Ian, and when his name flashed on the screen, my heart skipped into sprinting mode. He'd texted me.

You okay?

Yeah, I was okay. Sore in the feelings department, but okay. He didn't need to know all of that though.

Yeah. Sorry about today.

No problem.

I could hear his easygoing voice as I read those two words, and then suddenly I remembered...

Oh no. I left you with all those cupcakes!

A smiley face popped onto the screen. And then, *I handled it. No worries.*

Ian! I'm so sorry! What a jerk I was. I buried my face into Jeremy the Giraffe's neck and groaned. My phone buzzed again.

I could use some help getting them all to the barn tomorrow. Know anyone who could do that?

I raked my fingers through my hair and growled my name out loud—because remember? I lived alone and could do such things.

Yeah, the jerk who stuck you with all that work should definitely help you with that.

The three dots that indicated the other person was typing flashed on my screen, and then, *She's not a jerk.*

I didn't know what to say.

Kirstin, I don't think you're a jerk.

A sob suddenly rattled through me. Relief? Maybe, yeah. But also, still a little bit of disappointment. He didn't even mention the kiss idea, and while I should have been happy he was going to just skip over it like it hadn't happened and didn't matter, I wasn't.

Another buzz of my phone forced me to blink my eyes clear.

See you tomorrow?

And that was the end of it. We were moving on.

Yeah. I'll be there in the morning to help.

Good.

The end. Next story, please.

***

The back door to the bakery had a little bit of a squeak. I hadn't really noticed it before that Saturday, but it seemed to ring in my ears as I pushed it open, announcing my reentry into a world that really belonged to Ian and not me.

Last night, because I couldn't sleep, I painted an illustration of this kitchen. Ian was in the middle of it, juggling a giant spoon, a whisk, and an egg. In my mind, I saw me sitting on the counter, grinning and gooey eyed, and I wondered if I had looked at him gooey eyed for the past two weeks and hadn't realized it.

I didn't paint myself into that picture.

Ian looked over his shoulder at me from his place at the island, his trademark grin already in place. "Morning, sunshine."

"Morning." I hoped my smile didn't look as forced as it felt. "Started without me, I see."

He waved me over, and I stomped the snow off my boots before I headed toward his office to hang up my coat. He didn't follow me this time, which struck a flat note in my heart, because he always had before and had taken my coat from me to hang it up.

Guess things had changed.

I deposited my coat on the peg across from his desk and stopped on my way back to the kitchen, when I noticed my name written in Sharpie on a small box. My breath caught, and I reached for it.

A Dark and Dangerous.

What was I supposed to do with that? I mean, besides eat it, which I fully intended to, because what nut would waste one of Ian's cupcakes?

I shut my eyes and pulled in a long breath. If this was his way of weaving our friendship back to normal…

Sighing, I pressed my lips together and smothered that sudden sob that tried to push its way past my chest.

"Thanks for the cupcake," I said bravely, stepping back into his kitchen.

He paused his cupcake packing, one hand gripping a little confectionary heaven as it hovered over a box. "You're welcome." He looked back at me, and his smile seemed…different.

The connection between us as our eyes met made my heart puddle. This wasn't fair. Not at all. I stood rooted, unable to think past the numbness that connection had triggered. Ian looked back at the box he was filling, set the cupcake in his hand in its spot, and then turned back to me. Three steps narrowed the space between us, and he rubbed his hands against his jeans as he moved.

When he raised one of his hands, my imagination slipped into dream world, and I allowed the vision of him slipping his warm palm over my cheek, pulling my face toward his.

He didn't. Not in real life. Instead, his thumb tugged on the corner of my mouth. "It was supposed to make you smile."

"Oh." Surely he expected me to say more. I had nothing else though, because my head and heart were spinning and I couldn't think or feel straight. I must have managed a grin though, because he smiled back at me and then wiggled my arm.

"We have work to do."

"Yeah." The fogginess in my mind cleared a little bit, and I followed him back to the island counter.

It took two hours and four trips from the bakery to the barn to load and unload the six hundred cupcakes that looked amazing. Just like the guy who made them.

I faked my way back to lighthearted banter and was feeling pretty good about my acting until Ian asked me, as we finished setting up, if he'd see me that night.

Hadn't thought that far.

"You'll be here, right?" He tipped his head and waited for me to answer.

"Yeah. Representing Rock Creek Elementary's second-grade class. I'll be here." I didn't exactly have a choice. The whole Cupcake Dilemma was because of this dance that I was kind of expected to attend.

That was when reality crashed down on me. The Cupcake Dilemma was over.

Chapter 14

I debated about what to wear.

There was a pretty pink dress in my closet, waiting for such an occasion. It was girly and cute and perfect for a Valentine's Day date. I didn't have a Valentine's Day date, however, and the cold that had locked down on Rock Creek wasn't letting up. The barn would be warmer than the great freezing outdoors, but it was still a barn.

In my closet there was also a cute sweater tunic—something I'd worn in the classroom a few times—that paired nicely with skinny jeans and booties. Warmer. More practical. Less date-ish. All good reasons not to wear the dress.

My doorbell rang as I stood in my sweats in front of my bed, where I laid out both outfit choices. A little thrill zipped through me as I imagined Ian standing at my door, dressed in a swanky suit and holding a bouquet of Valentine's Day flowers.

Because he would do that.

Yeah. My head was such a mess. I face-palmed myself and muttered something like *stop being ridiculous* before I opened the door.

Not Ian. But I smiled anyway, because Anastacia stood with a bag of something draped over her arm.

"Hey there, girlfriend. Let me in. We only have like an hour before Mitch comes to pick us up."

"Us?"

"Yes, us. Did you think I was letting you go to the dance alone?"

"Well…" My lips closed, and I fished in the silence for a way out of this. Not that I didn't want to go with them, but I didn't want to be stuck there for longer than necessary.

Her right eyebrow arched. "Well…what? Wait. Maybe you have a *different* ride to the dance?" She winked.

"No. And please don't go there."

"Oh." Her shoulders sagged a little bit. "I just don't understand that man."

"I told you—he wasn't flirting. We're friends, and that should be okay. I'm trying to let that be okay. Okay?"

The expression on her face was somewhere between disapproval and disbelief, but then she brushed it away and smiled. "Okay. But you're still going to look amazing tonight, so let's get to work. Not that you don't always look amazing."

I blew out a little chuckle. Standing next to Anastacia Campbell, the model-worthy perky princess, I wasn't sure it was possible for anyone to look *amazing*, but it was sweet of her anyway.

She grabbed my hand and swept me to my room, stopping abruptly when she saw the clothes laid out on my bed. "Yes!" She unclasped my hand and lifted the dress as if it were the most beautiful thing she'd ever seen. "This. Is. Perfect."

"That's nice, but I'm wearing the tunic."

She molded a firm teacherish look. "Um, no. You are not."

"Uh, yeah, I am."

"This is too cute. You have to wear it. Ian won't be able to keep his eyes off you."

"See? Right there. That's why I'm not wearing it. And stop. You're not helping."

She tipped her head to one side and lifted an eyebrow. "Nothing wrong with—"

"No." I held a hand up.

"Come on, Kirstin. Wear it for you. If it snags Ian's attention, then bonus. But you obviously like the dress, because it's in your possession. So wear it. Don't let him stop you."

I suddenly understood how Mitch found himself entranced by the sweet persuasion of his wife. Who could say no to her kind smile and perfectly applied logic?

I caved, and she squealed, and for the next hour we were like high school girls getting ready for the prom. Curling irons and makeup and body spray and hair spray spread all over my bathroom countertop, and I found my real smile as Anastacia and I fixed each other's hair.

See? Life moved on. I was still me.

By the time Mitch came to pick up his wife, who looked amazing in her red sweater dress that highlighted the adorableness of her baby bump, and warm fuzzy boots, I felt more confident about going to the dance on my own.

I was good on my own. That was simple. Uncomplicated.

Mitch escorted Anastacia to the car, and I waved at them before they pulled away. I'd follow in just a few minutes. After I changed out of the dress and into the jeans and tunic.

Because I was fine on my own.

***

Ian found me immediately, which wasn't hard because I was stationed at the cupcake table. He took the spot beside me, and we kept busy chatting with people who came for dessert. Keegan Kent wandered over to us on his own, and even after he had his vanilla cupcake with heart sprinkles on top, he stood there grinning. At me.

"Bet you're gonna be sad when you have to leave Ms. Hill's class at the end of the year, aren't you, buddy?"

The boy didn't even blush, but I did. I elbowed Ian's side. He snagged my arm and held it.

"She could move up to third grade," Keegan said.

"That'd be fun. What do you think, Ms. Hill?"

I tried to glare at him, but his grin made my attempt turn upside down. "You're trouble. Did you know that?"

"No way. I make you smile. That can't be trouble."

Suzanna Rustin slipped up to the cupcake table, rescuing me from wherever this conversation was going to go. "Keegan, it's my turn for a dance." She held her hand out to him, and he smiled as if he were such a lady-killer. Suzanna laughed and rolled her eyes as Keegan tucked her hand under his arm.

What a charmer. He might be dangerous someday.

Sydney White wove her way to our table shortly after, her smile something I imagined Ramona Quimby would wear.

"Hey, fastest kid in the first grade," I said. "Have you had a cupcake yet?"

She made a show of glancing around. "I was waiting to see…"

"See?"

Her smile was followed by a nod. "Keegan gave me a thumbs-up. So they're good."

Understanding poked into me. "Ouch, Syd." I covered my heart as if she had actually wounded me.

Stepping around the table, she took my hand. "I'm just kidding, Ms. Hill. I already had one from my dad. It was really good." She gave me a thumbs-up and a full-toothed grin.

I side-hugged her and laughed. "Thanks. But Ian made them."

She seemed to not hear that part. "Are you two going to go dance?"

"What?"

"You should dance. This one's a fun song." Her look bounced from me to Ian and back again.

"Ian is a terrible dancer," I said, hoping that the heat on my face didn't show.

"Am not."

I whipped a raised eyebrow look to him. "Are to. I've seen it."

He held a hand out as if to make a bet, while over the speakers Josh Turner sang "Why Don't We Just Dance" to a solid rhythm, a steel guitar, and a piano. I reached to shake on it. Instead of betting, he tugged me toward him, and once we cleared the table, he spun me.

I tried to stop my chuckle. "You're going to cause an accident."

Backing to the dance floor, my hand in his, he winked. "Do you know how to swing?"

"Yeah. Don't think you do though."

He spun me out and then back in. Perfectly. His face sank near mine, and I felt my eyes widen.

"You ain't seen nothing." Mimicking Turner's crazy deep voice, Ian spoke while he moved me to a country swing.

I tipped my head back and laughed. And we danced. I didn't know if we were watched, and I didn't care. We were back to that place again. The fun one where Ian was a quirky goofball and I couldn't help but go along with it. The music ended, and we both stepped back, clapping even though the music wasn't live. Other couples around us applauded, and then the Rascal Flatts version of "Bless the Broken Road" started over the speakers.

Uncertain, I looked up at Ian. He cocked an eyebrow as if to ask me, but didn't wait for my answer before he stepped back toward me, his arms raised.

I tried not to think about the hand that curved around my waist and then warmed my back. Or the way he smelled like a strange and swoony combination of woodsy man and cake. Or the fact that he danced flawlessly.

Or the fact that I wanted so desperately to lean into his chest that *was right there in front of me* and feel those arms close around me, the rhythm of his heart tap against my face, and the weight of his head tip against mine.

Cupcakes and fairy tales. Guess I only got one. Wished I got to choose which. I would have picked Ian. Every single time.

We finished the dance and walked back to the cupcake table. Ian had been right—two hundred would have been woefully short. All six hundred of his generously donated cakes were gone. I no longer had a reason to stay.

Ian nudged my shoulder from behind. "Thanks for the dance."

I waited until my grin didn't feel wobbly before I looked back up to him. "You're full of surprises. Is there anything you're not good at?"

"You already know the answer to that." A blush brushed across his face, and his eyes lost the ever-present laughter. I couldn't read whatever serious thing he was trying to say to me in that look, but given that he didn't think it was funny, I figured it wasn't good. I didn't want to know.

I fingered the table. "Do they need help tearing down after this thing is over?"

"No, there's a sign-up for that. If you didn't put your name on it, you don't need to worry about it."

"Will there be enough help?"

"Had enough of me, huh?"

"That's not—" Well, it kind of was, but not the way he was implying.

His grin surfaced again, although not as big as normal. "It's okay, Kirstin. You've done a lot already. You don't need to stay if you don't want to."

Nodding, I scanned the barn, taking in the scene, snapping mental pictures to paint later. Tom and Andrea Kent smiling at one another as if they were new to love rather than sixteen years into their marriage. Joe and Kale White, him looking at her like he was still amazed she married him. Paul and Suzanna Rustin, dancing in perfect unison, one of his arms snaked around her and the other holding their snoozing little boy.

Snippets of life. I knew this small town had its dark side. Heard about how a banker had been dead set against Suzanna owning a piece of Rock Creek real estate and had landed himself into some personal and legal trouble in a crazy attempt to get rid of her. Knew that there was a reason for a sheriff in town, and that it was best to lock my doors at night and when I was away. The people of Rock Creek were still just people after all, and they came in all sorts. But in that moment, in that barn full of members of this town, I was proud to be included. To have a home in Rock Creek. Even if the love I saw between those couples sort of made my heart sore.

"Capturing ideas?" Ian's voice came from beside me, low and meant for only me.

"Some," I answered, knowing he was talking about my illustrations.

"I can't wait to see them."

I smiled, truly grateful that he'd brought this part of me out. "You will. Soon. Good night, Ian."

"Night, Kirstin." His fingers brushed my arm as I moved away.

I sort of wished I'd worn the dress. Not that I thought it'd have made a difference. But maybe…

Maybe it would have.

***

The snow had been falling since four. White covered the ground, the trees, the barn, and most relevant to that moment, the streets. My little Toyota Yaris was no match for the nearly eight inches that now blanketed the whole town.

I was stuck.

Snowflakes drifted down, twinkling in my headlights as if oblivious to the situation they were causing in my world. I sank back against the seat, shutting my eyes and wondering what to do. He'd help me. Not even a question. But as I sat there, "Bless the Broken Road" still playing in my mind, the dance we'd shared still tingling on my skin, I wasn't sure I could handle it.

And that was how he found me. Stuck in the snow, tipped back in my seat, dreaming about a different ending to this beautiful story. I hoped my thoughts didn't translate to my expression. Our friendship would never recover if I kept this up.

"Need a ride?" he asked.

"Or a push?" I countered.

"That's not happening. The car will be fine here—promise you won't be the only one not to make it out of the parking lot tonight. We'll come back for it after church tomorrow."

What else could I do? I nodded. And he held open my door, took my arm after I shut it, and guided me to his four-wheel-drive pickup. It was slow going to my house, but we made it, and when we got there, he shut off the engine.

I guessed he was hanging out for a while. Cool. I could be cool. I'd been cool all evening, right? We hung out quite a bit over the last several weeks. It'd be normal. I'd be normal.

I searched for normal while we walked into my little bungalow.

"What was that show you're addicted to?" Ian asked, wiggling out of his coat.

Normal hadn't shown his face, and I wasn't sure what Ian was talking about.

"Huh?"

"The one I'm not allowed to call you while you're watching. I need to see what's more important than talking to me."

"Oh. You want to watch that?"

"I assume you record them."

Duh. "Yeah but—"

"Start it up. I'll see if you have anything edible." He began searching through my cabinets.

If it had been anyone other than Ian, I would have been mortified, but given that he already knew my total kitchen ineptness, I merely shook my head.

"Ah. This'll work." He snapped a cabinet door closed and held a package of microwave popcorn.

I found that amusingly ironic. He tipped an eyebrow at my snort-laugh.

"Do you know how to use a microwave?" I asked, relieved that our sassy banter could be restored.

"Full of surprises, remember?"

I didn't touch that one, because it'd take me back to the dance floor, and I was just recovering from that. Instead, I found my show, and he employed the microwave, which still made me giggle—probably more than it should have, and then we were on the sofa, side by side, watching my girlie BBC drama.

The good thing about watching television together was that you didn't have to talk. I had nothing to say.

No, that wasn't true. I had words. Just not words that were going to take us back to the friend zone. They were more like...

Ian, I don't think I can do this. I like you too much. Why don't you like me? It seems like—

He nudged me, jarring me out of the speech I had unravelling in my mind. Pulling in a quick breath because he'd startled me, I glanced up at him.

Oh my word, why did he look at me like that? Eyes so deep and dark I thought I might die. He licked his lips, and then his fingers were in my hair, tucking the strands near my face behind my ear. What was he—

"I would have kissed you back."

I froze. The words, spoken in a husky, deep whisper, swirled in my mind, not making any sense. "What?"

The pad of his thumb traced over my top lip. "I would have kissed you back."

I studied him, my mind racing, trying to understand. Why hadn't he—

The thought cut off. Ian drew my face toward his until his breath warmed my mouth. "Don't believe me?"

"What?"

"Try it." His whisper seemed less serious, but still intimate. "See what happens."

His mouth so near mine. Fingers woven in my hair. There was only so much a girl could take.

I took the bait. Met his lips.

He kissed me back. And suddenly I didn't care what was on the TV, or the snow that had imprisoned my car, or why Ian hadn't just told me this last night. I was kissing Ian Connealy, and he was kissing me back. If the low groan that came from his throat was any indication, he was enjoying it as much as I was.

When his hold around me loosened and his kisses became lighter, thinking restarted in my brain. My first thought was, *Whoa. We were kind of making out there. Like teenagers.* Followed by, *At least we're not in a theater.* And then, *Why the heck didn't he—*

I finished the last one out loud. "Say anything last night?"

"What?" He smoothed my hair, which was probably a mess. His fault.

"You didn't say anything last night. Why?"

"You ran away."

"You could have followed me."

"I'd just put the last batch of cupcakes into the oven. You didn't give me a chance."

"But…" I searched his eyes, now feeling a little betrayed because didn't he have any idea how miserable I'd been for the past twenty-four hours? "You looked at me like I was crazy. And then today—"

"I was shocked. You hadn't given me any indication that you were—that we could maybe—" He shoved a hand through his hair and then rubbed his neck. "And then I thought Jeff told you, and I was kind of—"

"Jeff?"

His eyebrows pulled together, as if he didn't understand my not understanding. "Jeff Hanson. Your principal? He was my buddy in college."

Mr. Hanson. Mr. Hanson! Mr. Kirstin-you-can-handle-desserts-and-cupcakes-are-a-favorite Hanson! I stared at Ian, my lips gaping. "You set me up."

"Well, kind of. But not really. I mean—" He pinched my lips back together and then leaned in to brush them with his again. "Don't be mad. I really stink at this, remember?"

"I don't understand." Not surprising, mostly because every time his lips came near mine, I had a mental crash.

Ian leaned back, his hand cupping my face again. "I noticed you at the bakery and at the Christmas party in town. I knew you were a teacher, and I asked Jeff about you. He knew about my…uh, dating track record, so I guess he took things into his own hands. I didn't know until after he'd assigned desserts to you, but it felt like a safe plan. We could get to know each other, and then if things worked out, great. But if they didn't…no one got hurt. Or humiliated."

I raised my eyebrows. "I humiliated myself plenty."

His eyes…oh goodness, I stopped breathing again because those eyes turned dark and deep and said things to me that I'd hoped to hear but couldn't believe… "I thought you were adorable."

Thoughts. Coherent thoughts. Not about kissing.

That was a stretch. He was right there. And so kissable. I couldn't resist. But after one—or three—more lip dances, I pulled back again, having found the thought that needed to be voiced.

"You didn't say anything. You texted me last night. And today—we were together almost all day. Why?"

His grin settled, the lines by his eyes crinkling in the way that made him Ian—different from his twin brother, and exactly how I pictured him when he wasn't around. "I wanted both. This"—he dipped down for another quick kiss—"and the easygoing laughter. The fun we have. I wanted to make sure that wasn't gone."

He waited for me to respond, but I could only sit there, feeling ridiculously giddy under his tender gaze.

"Can we have both?" he asked, a little bit of pleading in his voice.

I smirked. "The baker wants to have his cake and eat it too?"

"I'm going to take that as a yes."

I guess my reaction to the kiss he pulled me into sufficed for my answer.

Jennifer Rodewald

Epilogue

Nothing changed that much. Except Ian called me *Sugar* quite a bit more than he ever did before—which would have been never. And he felt free to kiss me whenever he wanted. In the kitchen. Out on the street. At church. In the retail dining room of the Sweet Tooth. And on the playground at school. But that was only the one time—and it had a diamond attached to it, so that gave him a pass.

It was sweet—like Ian kind of sweet, which means sweet with a hefty balance of goofy tossed in for flavor. He'd enlisted my class for help, with Jeff's—his college-buddy-turned-my-boss—approval. One warm May day near the end of the school year when I had playground duty after school, several of my students came up to me in clumps, saying, "Ms. Hill! Come quick. There's a strange man over here, and we're not sure what he's up to."

That obviously got some attention. But every time I went to where they'd seen this "strange man," he'd disappeared. By the third time, I was seriously worried and called Mr. Hanson, who would then call the police. I assumed.

"Oh, don't worry about it, Kirstin. The school day's over. It'll be fine."

This was not a normal or acceptable response for a principal.

Unease twisted through my stomach as I debated what to do, but before I could dial the police, one of my students came running to me with a slip of paper flopping in her hand. "Ms. Hill! He left a note this time!"

She handed me the note, looking suspiciously not too concerned. I eyed her, unsure what to think of it, and then opened the note.

I will

That was it. In block letters, no punctuation. I will…
Murder you?

Take your children?

Hold you hostage?

I ran through the possibilities, trying to reconcile my student's behavior and this apparent psycho's intent. Another student came charging at me with another slip of paper.

love you forever.

I laughed—the relieved, I-feel-kind-of-dumb kind that comes out of your nose. Leave it to Ian. Also it was sweet, because he knew that was nearly exactly a line from one of my favorite children's books. I'd read it to him—Kleenex box nearby—and then through blurry vision, for the very first time told him that I loved him forever. That had been in March.

When Keegan came running up to me, hand clutched around a slip of paper, I smiled at him.

He grinned back. "He's okay, Ms. Hill. Unless you want to wait for me to grow up?"

"I'd be pretty old by then, Keegan."

He shrugged. "Yeah. That's what Ian said."

Thanks for that, Ian. I took the next note expecting it to be the next line from the book. He just skipped right over that part and went straight to the point.

As long as I'm living, my wife you will be.

"Huh," I said, mostly to the paper. "Presumptuous."

Keegan laughed. "He said you'd probably say something like that. Here." He held up another rolled-up slip of paper.

I unrolled it, finding one more word.

Please?

Ian came around the corner, his gaze zeroed in on me, that Dark and Dangerous—but in a good way—look fixed in his eyes. "Well?"

I glanced at Keegan, apparently making Ian panic a little.

"You gave her both notes, right, buddy?"

"She read them." Keegan held up both hands. "But if she's not gonna marry you…"

Looking back up to Ian, I grinned. "You want to marry me?"

"More than anything." His strides closed the space between us, and the question echoed in his eyes. "Are you gonna answer me?"

"You usually take my silence as a yes."

He lifted both hands, slid them around my head, and pulled me closer. "I need to hear you say it this time. Will you marry me?"

Of course I said yes.

Who knew the Cupcake Dilemma would end so yummy? Well, you did, probably. But me? Not really. And now, in just a few more weeks, I'll be Mrs. Ian Connealy. This total kitchen-fail girl will move into a loft that does not have a kitchen (dream come true) and start life with a baker who was a complete dating disaster.

Life is pretty sweet.

The End

Did you enjoy The Cupcake Dilemma? Please leave a review on Amazon, Goodreads, or your favorite online retailer! Thank you.

About the Author...

Jennifer Rodewald is passionate about the Word of God and the powerful vehicle of story. The draw to fiction has tugged hard on her heart since childhood, and when she began pursuing writing she set on stories that reveal the grace of God.

Jen lives and writes in a lovely speck of a town where she watches with amazement while her children grow up way too fast, gardens, and marvels at God's mighty hand in everyday life. Four kids and her own personal superman make her home in southwestern Nebraska delightfully chaotic.

She would love to hear from you! You can find her at:
https://authorjenrodewald.com
Facebook: authorjenrodewald
Twitter: @JRodes2
Instagram: author.j.rodes
or email her at jen@authorjenrodewald.com

Don't miss the other Rock Creek Romances!

Land of her own and the love of a good man.
Shouldn't that be enough?

Left wounded by a marriage cut short, Suzanna Wilton leaves her city life to start over in a tiny Nebraska town. Her introduction to her neighbor Paul Rustin is a disaster. Assuming he's as underhanded as the other local cowboys she's already met, Suzanna greets him with sharp hostility.

Though Paul is offended by Suzanna's unfriendliness, he can't stop thinking about her, which unsettles his peaceful life. A hard-fought friendship slowly kindles something more, but just as Paul's kindness begins to melt Suzanna's frozen heart, a conflict regarding her land escalates in town. Even in the warmth of Paul's love, resentment keeps a cold grip on her fragile heart.

Will Suzanna ever find peace?

WINNING TITLE FOR THE 2014 COTT OLYMPIA CONTEST

Someone has noticed me. A secret admirer? A man with a good heart, who sees how much I actually need help, even though I never admit it? Maybe this is the beginning of a beautiful story—a romance full of hope and second chances and love.

Maybe...

A secret Santa gift left on Kale Brennan's front porch opens up a fresh view of her ordinary life, and perhaps of God. Maybe she does matter. Maybe God sees her—as does a new-to-town music teacher who has her seven-year-old daughter gushing and her own knees buckling with his killer smile. But as Kale embraces new possibilities, a staple in her life—a man who is kind and steady, not to mention necessary for her injured daughter's recovery—also snatches her attention in an unexpected way. Will the one pursuing her with his secret gift and kind gestures be the one her heart longs for in the end?

"You could not possibly ask for more in a Christmas novella." -Katie Donovan, the Fiction Aficionado

Made in the USA
Middletown, DE
02 December 2018